The Mad Wizard

A Tarnished Lands Story

P.A. WIKOFF

Visit the author's blog pawikoff.wordpress.com

Patreon.com/pawikoff

Follow @pawikoff on Twitter and @p.a.wikoff on Instagram

Facebook.com/pawikoff

Edited by Crystal Wikoff. Copyedited by Cheryl Wikoff.

Cover art by my good buddy, Levon Jihanian

ISBN 978-0-9990058-4-2

This book is dedicated to every person who has tragically lost their life at the hands of a maniac.

Contents

Anticipations

The wind blows wildly through the castle streets with a loud whistle. Like an unforgiving river, it twists and churns through every corridor. What was once a rarity in these parts is now making up for lost time.

Racing shadows give the massive castle depth and texture as the clouds above move busily towards their next destination. Everything is in a hurry, and nothing has time to stop and smell the flowers. There is the occasional whiff of sweet scents and wonderous aromas, which dance by without regard for the senses they entice. Such is the case with a spicy sample of distant lands, filling the nostrils of a homebound man and pollinating his desire to explore.

So much has changed in such a short period of time. Even the newest of maps are outdated as of just a few months ago. It's a dream come true for cartographers, where work is often seasonal—following their employers' expedition schedules. However, it's quite cumbersome for the down-trodden treasure hunters who can't afford the newest, most updated printings.

This whole region has been in an age of re-creation, shifting and transforming in unusual ways. What was once a deforested wasteland incapable of supporting life is now a sea of shrubs and saplings ready to become a home for many smaller lifeforms in this new forever spring. The rest of the seasons have yet to re-surface and return home from their long-needed vacation.

The chirping birds don't mind and neither do the immigrants who have been flocking here faster than the fowl.

No one really knows why the forest started to regrow out of its own grave, but that doesn't stop many theories from surfacing. Some whispers have reported that it was the year-long rain, which washed away all despair and darkness that used to plague these parts. Others believe that the forest's roots fed off the corpses from the last apocalypse, and now they are finally full.

Superstitions are big in these parts, and no one dares to question this good fortune for fear that doing so would revert it back into another dark age—hot and dreadful.

Good news travels faster than bad. Once word got out about the fertile lands, farmers, prospectors, and entrepreneurs began arriving as fast as the wind could carry them—all seeking a better life rife with opportunity. Business is good and profits are even better for the residents who reside here.

To celebrate and pay homage to this time of rich beginnings, a show of harvesting has sprouted a new tradition. This harvest festival isn't only about trading fruit, herbs, and vegetables; it represents a new beginning for what was once thought to be forever lost. Hope, prosperity, and happiness are the three virtues celebrated on this joyous occasion. It is up to the painters, musicians, stage performers, magicians, combatants, and many other artists to showcase their talents while evoking the three virtues of the festival.

No matter if you seek entertainment or

revenue at the festivities, there's enough of everything for everyone in this land of abundance.

Although nothing lasts forever, especially good luck. If only life were that easy and things always went the way one imagines—simple and productive. But all this was in the past, before everything went upside down, before all the carnage...

Never Forget to Say Goodbye

"You never know what your last words are going to be until they clumsily fall out of you. You can spend a lifetime practicing and preparing, but it will never turn out quite as pretty as you expected or as poetic as you had hoped. It simply happens, and there is no going back for re-dos. More often than not, everything comes out heartfelt and meaningful through sheer emotion alone. Quoting the good-bye verse or re-creating a trembling farewell kiss will never do them justice. It's a true had to be there moment filled with silent screams and heavy eyes. It's the feelings behind the words that give them life as you're losing yours—as if your soul is transferring through vibrato breaths and holding on to a single moment in time for as long as possible.

"It is said that angels hear the voices of the dying, and on occasion they will even respond to them. The most precious thing to you will linger in your mind in your final moments. Those thoughts will pass on with you to the next life if truly spoken. No one will know what that thing will be until it arrives. It might be sentimental, selfish, humorous, or ironic.

"Unfortunately, more often than not, a shock will form within the departing, trapping their voice inside. Being robbed of your last words doesn't make them any less real, only much less memorable—especially by angels that might be within earshot. Like those fleeting moments, words are merely the vessel bringing feelings to life. No one ever remembers a poet's scribe verbatim—only their own reaction to the words and how it warmed their soul.

My final word was 'oops,' and I wish no one had heard me utter it. It is something I would never want to be remembered by. But as I transcend between life and death, I suddenly don't care about the land of the living.

"The fleeting moments that pass quietly between transitions are often forgotten. To be remembered or recognized in someone's finality is to be immortalized with good fortune. Never wait to express yourself to those you care about the most, because shame burns off of the fuel we call procrastination." *-Stable Master Brawn, age 43.*

Day Four, 10:08 am: Hide with Pride

Kip grabs his head, trying to make himself as small as possible. Where did it all go wrong? How did it even begin? Light creates new shadows from a new day. The darkness might be gone, but the horrors on the outside very much remain. Who knows if or when the sorrowful sounds will be granted the merciful peace of silence.

He doesn't want to see the aftermath any more than he wants to believe it all to be real. How long will this travesty go on? Forever, perhaps? After three days of this, there seems to be no end in sight. How long can his ears endure the terrible sounds that echo throughout the dark hallways? How far can his nerves take the unimaginable power that shakes the castle walls endlessly? Or how much can his nose taste the smell of death that is everywhere and quickly turning to rot?

Going over the past in his mind is his only way to find the clues he so desperately seeks. His recollection is shaken and fuzzy, and having endured days without much sleep, his tiredness is only making matters only worse. This is a huge puzzle that needs to be solved. He has but one desire, to put an end to everything that is transpiring or, at the very least, escape this destruction with his life intact. If only he could gather enough courage to poke his head outside, but that would mean risking it getting blown off. Firmly resting on his shoulders is where he likes it to be.

The blood that once covered his body has long since turned cold and dry. Until forced to move, Kip is paralyzed with fear, shaking uncontrollably—matching the castle's rumbling. Maybe the massive structure is just as frightened, he wonders.

Think coward, Kip repeats to himself, hoping his mind will start obeying him again. It is hard to come up with anything clever when an electric sound is crackling and burning endlessly just outside these walls. He knows the power of such a noise and the implications of being on the receiving end of such force.

Now it acts the same as a rattlesnake's tail, a warning to stay away—far, far away. Only, it's getting closer with each passing minute. Soon it will come for him, like it has come for so many before him. He has to devise something foolproof; a plan of escape or heroism. Instead he just sits there, like a soon-to-be corpse.

"Come on, you have to do something," Kip says to himself through chattering teeth.

"Shhh, be quiet!" a child reprimands.

He is a grown-up, hiding in the underbelly of the castle among children in the dusty storage room. He should be out there with the guards, heroes, and adventurers—though he has seen too much, witnessed things that no goodly person should ever have to. If he didn't care so much, he might be able to force out one last act of bravery.

Someone has to come by to protect these children. If not for them, for him. He is much too broken to tend to them himself. Maybe he can go out and find that person; but what if there is no one left? No, he will stay put for the time being until he thinks of something, anything...

Day Two, 2:03 pm: A Couple of Fools

The sun is winding down across the horizon, and the birds are still jubilant, enjoying the festival as much as anyone. People everywhere are in high spirts, except for one man, Kip.

Things haven't gone exactly how he had anticipated. One thing is clear, he needs the help of his companion. After hours upon hours of no sales, or any interest in his table in general, Kip is forced into a role of people-watching. People in extravagant hats and costumes are masquerading around, seeking admiration and general attention. During the festival, everyone can be anyone else, if only for a day or two. No one comes as they are; they become who they'd like to be. There are a couple of true heroes among the fakers. Side by side, you can easily tell the difference between chainmail ringlets and the painted cloth impostors, but at a distance they look nearly identical. Oftentimes the replica weapons are sharper than the real thing. Though after one swing, an experienced fighter will find that their weight is all wrong, and the source material isn't sturdy enough to parry an attack. It is a dangerous thing to have a weapon whose looks are better than its practicality and use.

Kip, however, came as himself. He has no hero costume to distract him from his mission, although hiding behind a platemail helm is exactly what he would love to do right about now.

More than a dozen times today, someone has come up to him and tried to guess his costume. One person thought he was going as some famous stable boy, another thought he was dressed as a woman. On three separate occasions, he was asked if he was a eunuch. This type of attention felt worse than being invisible.

"Would you like a tip?" a strange whisper says from out of nowhere.

Kip nearly jumps right out of his skin upon feeling the sudden warm breath against the back of his neck. "Uhh, sure. I mean...Hello?" Straining his neck, Kip turns to face the woman who is uncomfortably close to him.

"Hiya. This is what I do to bring people over to my table..." she says at a normal volume this time around.

Kip gives her an encouraging nod, patiently waiting for her to finish her sentence.

To his surprise, she doesn't. Instead, she just grins at him as if frozen in time.

He is confused. Is there something he isn't

quite getting, like a prank or joke? A few moments pass by uneventfully.

"Okay, I'm game. Tell me." Again he waits for her to explain her master sales plan in depth, but she just sits there like a happy little statue.

"I am doing it right now. All you have to do is smile."

"That's it? Just...smile?" Kip was hoping that she was going to reveal some secret foolproof tactic that will guarantee him a better sales rate, not something he does naturally without even trying.

"Yes, but there is a little more to it."

Now you're talking. Kip rubs his hands together in delight.

"First you need to lock eyes with them like this." The woman stares into Kip's eyes as if she is looking directly into his mind. It is almost intrusive. "Then just smile." She has a lovely set of white teeth, which really soften the intensity of her stare.

"Woah," Kip says, mesmerized.

"One more thing. Whatever you do, don't look away. If you turn, or even blink, they will use it as an opportunity to run. But if you keep their gaze steady, it will draw them in like a fish caught on a line," the woman explains, finishing with a cute little wink.

"I can't do that last part. No way."

"I know. I throw that in for the cute ones."

Kip feels his face turn flush. Is she flirting with him?

"That's it. Try it out and see for yourself."

At first he was skeptical, but when she really got down to business, her smile *was* quite welcoming. He mulls over the whole thing and starts to buy in to her tactic. This isn't going to be some easy task. Kip will have to spend quite some time practicing this little maneuver if he wants to get it right.

"Tha..." Before he can thank her, she is skipping back across the way to her perfume and candle display. Perhaps he took too long internalizing this whole encounter.

Is it really that easy, he ponders. *Am I not welcoming enough? I smile as much as the next guy.*

Sure, smiling more is definitely something he can add to his sales routine. What does he have to lose anyway?

Over and over again, he works on the perfect smile. The hardest part is trying to make it seem genuine and not forced.

"This is hard work. I guess I don't smile enough," Kip says, rubbing his sore face.

After a good twenty minutes of working out his cheek muscles, he is ready.

Dozens of people pass by, but Kip is waiting for the perfect moment to strike. After a minute or two, a friendly-looking man glances slightly at his table.

It is time.

First Kip locks eyes with the man, never blinking—and setting the bait. Then he tries to mimic the woman's welcoming smile, bearing all his front teeth, top and bottom rows.

Puzzled, the man hesitantly returns his gaze after hedging slightly.

It is working. This is the most interest he has had at the festival thus far. There is no room for mistakes, Kip knows.

The man quickly spins around, as if to see who Kip is *really* smiling at. When he realizes that he was not mistaken, and the creepy sales-man is looking at *him*, the man puts up his hand to block his face while he speed-walks away as fast as possible.

Slowly, Kip's happy face turns into an open-mouthed frown.

This is humiliating and much worse than

being ignored all day. All he can do is hope that the woman didn't see it.

He glances across the way, and the woman and her neighbor are both smiling and giving him an encouraging wave.

"Of course they saw it. My mouth was open wider than a chasm," Kip mumbles to himself.

Now it is her turn. Just like how she explained, she mimics the exact move she did on him. Instantly, some guy walks right up to her display and leans on her table flirtatiously. It worked. Everything went exactly the way she said it would. The guy even seemed to resemble a fish in the way he waddled over to her.

She gives Kip a coy wink.

Kip can't help but wonder why the move didn't work for him. *Oh, right, I'm not a cute girl.*

Going back to his old ways of people-watching, Kip notices that everyone else seems to be having a grand old time...except one man. He seems to be just as out of place as Kip himself. Shoulders scrunched, his eyes are darting to the floor to avoid everyone's eye contact.

"That guy looks like I feel," Kip observes quietly, "but worse."

The man is dressed in dark robes, and when

he puts up the hood to shroud his head, the wind keeps blowing it off. After the third time of trying to conceal his face, the man gives up on the task altogether. He is circling around, trying to stay a safe distance away from the crowds of people. It almost looks like a child's game of sorts, but this man is no child. He just wants to get through the people without brushing up against anyone.

"But why?" Kip wonders.

Right when the man makes a little headway, he has to retreat back to avoid a stumbling party-goer or a self-centered businessman, each of whom nearly walks over him.

Suddenly, the man catches Kip staring, and they lock eyes—and not in the way the woman described. It is alluring, but in a haunting sort of way.

Startled, Kip stands up, bracing himself on his table.

Kip considers flashing the man a welcoming smile to reel him in, but on second thought, he doesn't have the courage. Not after that last rejection. Kip feels immense fear and sadness from the man as their look lingers. Fear and sadness are two emotions that Kip has had to battle within his own struggles, and he knows them well. Buried deep behind the man's eyes is a juvenile undertone with deep, unequivocal sadness. This is one troubled individual.

Kip gets the impression that this *boy* is somehow trapped inside a man's body. Age never makes a man; it is forged through experience and duty. All Kip knows for certain is that this person is terrified and alone, like a frightened child lost from his parents. Their shared moment is almost a cry for help. No, it is one, although Kip doesn't know if it is the man's or his own. They are caught in each other's stare, but who is the fish and who is the fisherman?

Kip wants to go talk to the man to better understand their connection, but to say what exactly, he isn't sure.

Unfortunately, Kip will never know, as some customers approach him and walk right in front of his line of vision, breaking their intimate staring contest.

It's a middle-aged couple—with their arms interlocked. They go together like a pair of old boots. Both seem quite comfortable sharing each other's space.

Kip, however, isn't comfortable sharing his own space. An old feeling starts to come over him, and he tightens his jaw to keep it at bay, a technique he uses to slay anxiety when needed.

Not wanting to seem angry or at all unpleasant, Kip knows a greeting is in order. Torn between waving and extending his arm, he awkwardly twitches his hand. Finally, he decides to use his words instead. "Can I help you with anything in particular?" Kip asks, flashing the whites of his teeth, hoping this time it doesn't drive anyone off in a hurry.

"What is it that you're selling?" the woman asks, adjusting the freshly-cut flower in her hair.

Mesmerized by the blooming scent, Kip closes his eyes and takes in its splendor. What he should be doing is asking her about her affinity towards flowers to make a connection before hitting her with his sales pitch. Instead, he is swept off in the flower's glory.

"Weeds, obviously," the man chimes in, pointing at the sign, breaking Kip out of the moment.

"Stop that," she says, tapping him on the chest playfully.

"He isn't completely wrong," Kip admits, holding his hand out to his display.

"See, I told you. Let's go." The man unlinks his arms from the woman, who isn't budging.

"Don't tell me what to do." The woman's face turns sour as if she just ate a lemon.

"You heard him. It's a waste of time."

"Now hold on."

"For what?"

"I don't like how you're talking to me."

"If I may..." Kip tries to interject, offering a biting berry sample.

"Stay out of it!" they both say in unison.

Kip feels like a turtle slinking back into the safety of his shell after getting scolded in such a public way. No one likes to be in an argument, especially one you're losing, but witnessing a conflict you aren't even invested in is its own special torture.

Some think of him as being anti-social or even a bit weird, but attention isn't something Kip ever desires. And if the attention he is getting happens to be negative, he might as well disappear altogether. For Kip, this is the last place he would like to be, currently.

"Look at all this stuff. It's total garbage. I spend two months a year ripping that invasive stuff off our land, and now you want to purchase some? I can't believe you," the man says, shaking his head back and forth.

"Now, now. I never said I was going to buy a

thing. But if I were, it's my coin. You can't tell me what to do with it or how to spend it."

People are staring, and Kip's vision is starting to tunnel. "If you want my opinion..."

"No one asked you!" the man barks at Kip with an intimidating voice. He returns to the spat without skipping a beat. "Really? Your coin? If I didn't pay all your expenses, you wouldn't have any coin left for extravagances, let alone these so-called plants. Either way you look at it, I'm paying for those things one way or another."

"Oh, yeah? Is that how you feel about it?"

"Don't get me started."

"Oh, I think you're quite beyond just 'getting started,' husband," the woman says incredulously. Her shaky hands peruse through her change purse. "How much for this one?" She motions towards a bite-berry bush with a raise of her eyebrows.

"Uh, it isn't really for sale. It's more of a decoration."

"I don't care. I'm buying it," she says in protest with a shrug.

"Unbelievable!" The man throws up his arms in disgust as he starts to storm off, then suddenly turns around to solidify his final words. "Come find me when you remember why you married me." And with that, he disappears into the dense crowd of people.

His words anger her to the point where they cause her to drop her change purse, spilling out its contents—coins of all different sizes, shapes and values—on the table.

"I may never know why I made that huge mistake!" The woman clenches her fist, trying to bottle up all of her anger.

Kip quickly scrounges around, collecting all of the monies before they are lost among the cobblestones of the floor. One copper piece nearly rolls off the table, but his agile hand catches it midflight.

She is too entrenched in her argument to thank Kip for his quick hands.

"Are you okay?" Kip asks sincerely, returning her coins, which he managed to stack into a little tower in his hand.

"Yes...I mean, I will be. He just makes me so mad sometimes. I feel like I have to ask permission to spend my own money. Am I crazy? You agree me with me, don't you?" Reluctantly, she reclaims her coins with a wave of her hand.

"I couldn't begin to give you advice on relationships," Kip admits, pushing the berry plant across the table to her. "Here, keep it. Just know that their seeds can be dangerous."

"No, let me pay you for it."

"Actually, this event is supposed to be moneyless. I am not allowed to accept anything other than vouchers. Plus, I'm more in the business of buying than selling anyway."

"Really? What are you in the market for?"

Kip's head disappears underneath the tablecloth as he rummages through his secret stash.

While waiting for Kip to return, the woman glances over her shoulder for her husband among the sea of people. Her forlorn look portrays a verse from a sad poem directly from her broken heart.

"Here it is." Kip delicately holds up a green orb between his two hands. He cradles it, showing how important it is to him. This is the whole purpose for him being here, to acquire more of these. To most people in these parts they're worthless, but to Kip they're everything.

The woman's eyes barely look back at him. "Oh, I think I've seen those before. It's a seed, right?"

"It is more complicated than that, but...yes, I guess you could say that. Where did you see one?" Kip presses, hoping she is mistaken.

"There is one in our barn. We talked about planting it but never got around to it. Figures...just like him to never finish any projects around the house then act like I'm the lazy one."

The feeling of hope that Kip once had instantly leaves him. He thought this was going to be his last year, but he can't be further from the truth, not with more pits sitting around in people's barns.

"All this fuss over nothing...buying stuff." she scoffs.

"Is it possible to buy it off you, like if I come to your lands?" Kip asks, still grasping at the hope of completing his long quest.

"What? Oh, yeah, sure." The woman lets out a pouty-lipped sigh.

"Great, I could come by tonight if you live in the region, or maybe in a couple days if that works better for you," Kip trails off, caught in the excitement of the find.

"Forgive me, I'm not in the right headspace right now. Here, for your trouble." The woman tosses Kip a silver coin, forgetting about the pit.

Kip looks around, hoping no one noticed money changing hands. He can get thrown out if someone were to see, but he just doesn't have the heart to tell her.

"At least take this." Kip stands, extending the plant that started all this drama.

"I better not. If he sees that thing, it will surely send him into a rage. But thanks for listening." She musters a fake smile, and like that, she too is lost in the crowd.

Day Two, 8:08 pm: I'm So Sorry

As the panic goes into full swing, Kip feels disoriented as he tries to find his way in the midst of everything. The air is stale and as thick as molasses. Time, direction, and all logic seem to be out the window currently. There is too much going on to process any of it. It is like his mind is having a sensory overload.

There is an endless blur of people dashing in every which direction, with no order to their escape. Kip can't decide whom to follow and whom to avoid.

Pacing back and forth, Kip mumbles to himself for clarity, "What's going on? No, no, this is not real. This is an illusion or a dream." Without thinking of the consequences, Kip pinches himself on the arm. "Son of a bastard!"

It hurts much more than he thought it

would. Surely, this isn't the first time he has pinched himself, but somehow he is more sensitive to it right now.

The whole world around him suddenly disappears, and all he can do is focus on the throbbing pain he caused himself. He wonders how something so small could produce such a vast sensation. Either his fingers are much stronger than he ever thought possible, or his skin is the weakest, most pathetic thing in the world. Deep down, Kip knows the truth. It is on the edge of his exhaling breath when something snaps him out of admitting it aloud.

Off in the distance, he sees a sinister grin illuminated by soft candlelight. No wait, it's laughter. How could anyone find humor in such a dire situation? Kip touches his own face, realizing that the maniacal man is looking directly at him. "Why is he laughing at me like I'm a jester? I didn't even do anything." Kip stands up with a shrug and a quizzical look upon his face.

As if things couldn't get any worse, a repetitive banging sound suddenly echoes throughout the area. There is no way of know ing where it is coming from.

Faster than a loose arrow, Kip hits the deck.

He's never heard such a loud, abrasive sound in his life, and it gives his ears an instant ringing to remember it by.

After a beat of silence, he peers out from between his trembling fingers. The surrounding candlelight has all been blown out from the continuous bursts. It is now much too dark to see anything, but there seem to be far less people moving about than moments before. Using his best judgment, the danger appears to be coming from everywhere!

In rapid succession, the dreadful sound starts up again. This time Kip holds his face in dismay, keeping his eyes wide open so that they can bear witness to what exactly is happening. Strobing bursts of light appear in unison with the sound—illuminating the horror at every turn. Wounds mysteriously appear on the fleeing people and drop them like flies. The wet sounds of the holes forming on their victims make Kip cringe.

Some unseen force is attacking the festival. Shards of debris fill the air as projectiles collide with wooden carts and anything more malleable than the castle walls. Everything that isn't destroyed ricochets the debris off into a random direction, leaving nowhere safe out there.

In the middle of all the chaos, Kip spies something out of place.

"Honey! Where are you?" a woman with a large, red flower in her hair screams. She is frantic. "I didn't mean any of it. I want to be married to you." She looks left and right, ignoring the deadly projectiles that are whizzing by her with great speed.

The smart people are taking to the ground, scattering against the walls and finding cover in the shadows, their bulk filling up all the darkness.

While everyone else is taking refuge, the woman is taunting the power out in the open, fearing not for her own safety. "I take back everything I ever said!" she continues. She must have guardian angels watching over her, because she is the only one left standing. Her white dress is dusted with red from the air around her as blood and life take to the night's sky.

To stand up and look death in the eye because life isn't worth squat without your other half—that is a sentiment to swoon over. Kip recognizes the brave woman from prior in the day, not from her raspy voice but from the wilting flower tucked behind her ear. Earlier it was fresh and beautiful. Now it seems to reflect to-day's events perfectly.

I thought they would have made up long before now, Kip thinks to himself.

It shouldn't make a difference, but because he remembers speaking to her, he is more invested in helping her. Everyone is in the same tragedy, but her anguish is putting him the most on edge. It reminds him of a time when someone he was quite fond of left this world. Kip was much too weak to do anything then, and nothing has changed now. He doesn't want to think about it or live through it again this time.

Mother always used to tell me, "Kippy, you're much too nice for this unforgiving world," he remembers, while trying to think of something else—anything else to distract him from watching this woman die. *I will not cry.*

"I still remember why I married you. How could I forget?" the woman says with a chuckle.

Something rips a hole through her loose-fitting dress. Either she doesn't notice or doesn't care.

It is much too close for Kip's comfort.

She just continues on as if nothing else in this world matters. "It was your kind smile that made me feel at home, even though I never had such a place to call my own. That is what you gave me," the woman confesses.

The scene is eerie and heart-wrenching to witness. Only moments ago, there was a horde of people. Now there is nothing but the lonely woman and piles of fallen bodies. All eyes that are left witness are on her, fixated on her plight while the magical sound continues to assault their eardrums.

"I knew at that moment..." she says.

Be careful. Kip reaches for her, but his words are kept at bay by fear. With all his being, he wants to get up and help reunite the couple, not for himself, but for what they represent— something lost, true, and beautiful. Except he doesn't. Instead, he slowly pulls back his hand and slinks into what cover he has behind a broken potted plant, its dirt spilling out underfoot. Nearly sick, Kip watches her pain from the safety of his protective spot, feeling like dirt himself.

"Call me easy, but that was all it took," she says fondly, wiping a tear of happiness from her eye.

There are some whispers of encouragement from the other spectators. They are urging her to find cover and stop being so foolish. But love isn't about playing it safe or convenient; it's about grand gestures, and this is hers.

"I want to apologize—to say I am truly sorry. Funny, huh? I bet you never thought you'd hear me say those words together." For a moment, the woman's face lights up as she remembers her dear husband. "I do mean it," she continues, although her beloved doesn't seem to be there to respond.

Maybe it is too late for him to accept her apology. The thought brings a chill down Kip's spine. He is rooting for her, for them, for love—everyone is. Kip's heart lurches for the woman and her pain. He knows that there is no one in this world he could ever care that much for.

Heroes are Made

"To be dignified is to feel another's pain and sacrifice as your own, to mourn and grow. I've always had a hard time coming to grips with the last part of this concept. Pain pulls against my sympathy, but the empathy never subsides. In silent remembrance of loss, it forever lives inside the scar of my broken heart. To forget is to abandon humanity and live a life not worth living. These are the principles that heroes abide by and cowards overlook in lieu of their own self-interests. I am neither one nor the other. I have no riches, but I live adjacent to some wealthy folks, indeed. I live in the background, as an overlooked object.

Villains are just misunderstood champions seen through a different lens. Both sides are the other's opposite, fighting for a cause and against the opposition's oppression. I've been on either side, and the view is very much the same. Who's to say which side is right and which side is wrong, what is good and what is bad. The bodies pile up equally on both sides in the struggle of righteous rightness.

No one knows how or why the killing started, but I will remember the moment it ended—at least when it ended for me.

"During my life, I have seen a lot of things and been told a lot of stories. I fitted the young, I fitted the old—I once adorned a queen with a glorious crown. In all my years, I've learned one truth: no matter their creed or stature, the laces always pull the same." *-Handmaiden Bella Rouse, age 53.*

Day Two, 9:15 pm: The Adventuring Party

Inside the castle tower, Kip finds refuge from the outside ailments. It isn't the largest or even the tallest of the fortress's peaks, but it is still standing, and that is enough. The outside violence is muffled by the thick blocks of stone, though pressing his hand against the wall, Kip feels the horror through the vibrations. He jerks his hand away quickly, as if he touched something painfully hot. Things are not great out there. In fact, they seem to be getting worse.

Sharing the sanctuary with Kip is over two dozen or some-odd attendees who are preparing to run with him towards the danger.

The torchlight gives everyone an ominous glow that sets the tone for the events of the day. Among them are brave warriors, performers, and just plain everyday folks who have taken it upon themselves to stand up and fight whatever is out there, instead of hiding or giving up.

Kip feels almost fraudulent being among such a courageous lot. He only chose this path after seeing what horrible things were happening to those who tried to flee. Running from the threat only left them open to getting hit in the back. No, Kip wants to see what is coming at him. It is his only chance of escaping death. Fraudulently or not, he is here, and he will try to help in any way that he can—if he can.

"Let's pool our resources and see if we can get everyone equally outfitted for battle," a lean blond man announces, relinquishing two daggers and a fine-looking short sword into the center of the room.

"Who made you the leader?" a bearded man asks, hugging his shield tightly.

"My name Taarl, of the swampmen. I only aim to help those who are less fortunate than myself, for the survival of us all, not to decree commands." With a balled-up fist, he strikes his palm eagerly.

"I would die before taking orders from a man of the swamp," the bearded man retorts. He reaches for the hilt of the weapon on his back but doesn't unsheathe it, not yet.

A couple of heads shake back and forth in disagreement with the bearded man's seemingly narrow-minded words, though it is nowhere near the majority. The swamp people have a reputation for unsavory living conditions, and the rumors about the food they consume is beyond disgusting. Then there is the smell, but that stereotype mostly comes out of the mouths of xenophobes. Even Kip has heard such tales in the far-off reaches of his homeland, and he has never even seen a swamp to speak of.

"Let me repeat, I don't mean to bark orders or rule anyone. There is no need to have more weapons than number of hands to wield them," Taarl elaborates, outstretching his arms to further press his point.

"I have two shields, and I need them both!" a voice from the crowd barks.

"If that is your fighting style, so be it," Taarl says.

"As a matter of fact, it is," the shield hoarder says proudly.

Tilting his head between two stocky people, Kip spies the man with the shield situation. One is a small buckler resting on his forearm. Bucklers are often used for close, one-on-one combat. The other is a large tower shield that rests on his back, spanning the length of his neck to knee. Most likely this one is used for ranged attacks or mounted combatants. Surely, he doesn't need to watch his back with that thing stowed behind him. In a sense, his auxiliary shield is doubling as armor, even though he isn't exactly using it, thus proving his argument.

"Fair enough. Again, I am not commanding. I am merely suggesting on a case-by-case basis," Taarl reiterates.

"Where are all the guards? Shouldn't they be dealing with this threat?" Kip asks out of turn. It must have been his nerves, but his voice never sounded so high-pitched before.

He gets a lot of sideways glances from the room as it falls silent for a brief moment.

"I watched them flee for their lives like a bunch of scared donkeys," a female voice says, sticking out her tongue in disgust.

"Not true. I saw one helping a cripple get out of harm's way," Taarl counters.

Kip admires the swampman for taking charge and trying to unite the group. He is tall and charismatic, two traits that Kip has always wanted to have, but his parents' genes were to blame for at least one of those. He comes from a long line of "pocket people" as they were often insulted—small and forgettable. Deep down, Kip would do anything to take command and save the day. It pains him to sit idly by and watch bad things happen. Except, what if he were to steer everyone in the wrong direction? People could die or get seriously hurt due to his inexperience. He couldn't live with that outcome. No, that is a risk he could not take. Instead, he watches Taarl with awe-filled eyes.

"I don't care what the guards are up to. If they're not here, they don't matter. We cannot spare any time squabbling on this point. We have to focus on things we can control," an agile-looking woman says, petting her large and ferocious looking feline companion.

A man jumps back at the sight of the vicious beast as if he just noticed the thing purring at her side.

Someone from the crowd throws a spool of rope into the pile. "This is all I can spare. Don't ask me for more."

"Thank you. That's a start," Taarl says with a half grin, showing how glad he is that he reached at least one person.

"I need all my weapons. They're sentimental to me," announces the bearded man.

"Look, no one said you have to give up your possessions. I only suggested that someone less fortunate might be able to borrow some equipment, if you can spare it."

"Spoken like a true thief," adds the bearded man.

"You're not being helpful. Look at this guy here," Taarl points squarely at Kip, drawing everyone's attention to him. "He wouldn't stand a chance out there alone with no weapons, armor, or proper footwear." Just like that, the man Kip looks up to turns on him, using him as an example of what not to do.

Nearly in unison, every head in the room looks down to get a glimpse of the leaf wrappings Kip has tied to his feet with twine.

"What? It is part of my costume," Kip lies, trying to play off his attire. The truth is that he lost his shoes while in a drunken stupor. He planned on buying something better, but the cushy leaves were quite comfortable and airy.

"Those are rough, even by swamp stand-ards. Right, Taarl?" a random person in the crowd says, attempting to be humorous.

Suddenly, flying out of the mass of people in a wide ark are a pair of leather boots. They land near the spool of rope with a thud.

"See, that is very helpful. Thank you, anon-ymous donor," Taarl says, picking up the footwear and extending them to Kip.

Frantically, Kip shakes his head back and forth, not wanting the charity. "Uh, no. I don't need anything. I will be quite fine, really." Then he wonders if he's giving away his bravery ruse. As a last-ditch effort, he makes two fists, trying to appear menacing. "I can fight in these. I do it all the time," he says in a low voice that cracks halfway through the sentence.

Disappointing groans erupt from the group as they witness Kip's poor attempt at being fierce.

Someone no taller than a boy and slightly

smaller than Kip approaches with a concerned look upon his face. "Not like that," he whispers, pulling Kip's thumbs out from the center of his fists. "You're going to break a bone if you swing like that."

Uproarious laughter ensues at his expense.

Kip's face is as red as an ember and just as hot. He is completely humiliated by the mockery—even if the boy was only trying to help.

Slowly, Kip hides his hands behind his back, bested by a child.

"Arming those who have no proper training is going to get a lot of us killed!" the bearded man announces with booming inflections.

There might be some truth in his words, though they're hard to swallow, especially for Kip, who is currently the object of all of their attention. Even if he were trained in such weapons, it is true he doesn't have the courage, strength, stamina, or anything else that goes along with being a man of battle. Kip once nearly killed himself trying to chop wood with an axe. He still believes wholeheartedly that it was the axe's fault, but that is neither here or there.

"Come on, everyone. We have to work together until we find out what is going on out there," a well-armed woman says, dropping a short spear in the pile. "He can use it—or anyone else; I really don't care."

"We can always loot the little guy when he proves worthless," a man wearing an extravagant bell-lined hat says, jingling as he talks.

"It might actually be a good way to stash some back-up weapons around the battlefield," a voice echoes from underneath their steel helm, which completely obstructs the fighter's face.

This logic causes quite a few nods and accepting moans from the crowd.

"Isn't it bad luck to take a weapon off of a corpse? I mean, it wasn't lucky for them," Kip adds, trying to defuse this whole thing. This is actually a real superstition where he comes from. People are buried with their weapons as an act of eliminating the spread of bad luck among the living.

"Nonsense. There is no such thing as luck. Nobles invented the concept to divert blame away from them," someone interjects while sharpening a sickle-bladed staff.

"You cannot punish a sword for its owner's lack of skill," someone else adds.

"Don't be nervous; you'll make a fine

corpse," the bearded man says with a hardy laugh.

Great. I'm not worth more than being a dead weapon storage, Kip thinks to himself.

It seems this plan is acceptable to most. One after another, people of all equipment levels and stature glance at Kip before adding some armor, weapon, or other piece of gear into the ever-growing pile. Each contribution is paired with a nod to Kip, as if they are giving it to him personally.

Feeling put on the spot, he awkwardly thanks each one for their donation as a way of deflecting the feeling. But this only increases the sense of charity and makes the feeling worsen inside him.

Most people add at least one item into the stash, though some drop two or three. One man drops a jeweled halberd and is met with 'oohs' from the crowd. Everyone seemed to donate something, except the bearded man who is stubborn and loud with his protest.

Once the pile is complete, the crowd circles up and eagerly waits for Kip to make his selection.

He just stands there, dumbfounded. This pile is dangerous, with spikes and points sticking every which way, like a metal hedge-hog. It would prove quite unfortunate if Kip happened to hurt himself while choosing a weapon for his own protection. That would be just his luck. *How horrible would the owner of that weapon feel if that were to happen? Plus, what good is a corpse mule if it dies before it has a chance to stretch out its legs?* These are a few of the thoughts that are racing through Kip's head while he stares blankly at the hoard.

Prudently Kip approaches the pile, knowing it's now or never. Suddenly he feels small again, less than a person, less than himself, less than a child. A nervous tic develops on his face. He can't fight it, not with all these people staring at him.

"My oak crossbow is in there. It is very light-weight and blindingly accurate," one medium-built adventurer suggests.

"Go on." Kip feels a shove in the small of his back from another person.

All eyes are on him as he moves in closer to the pile.

Kip fears that whatever he takes will limit someone else from using the equipment. He knows himself, and the odds of him using any of this stuff is slim to none. He couldn't possibly hurt someone, even if it were in self-defense.

The pressure is so much for him. Trying to get through this experience as fast as possible, Kip starts to rummage through the pile carefully. The first thing his hands procure is the spool of rope. "Can I take this?"

"Well, sure, but you need something a little deadlier, like this hand axe here," a man who is shorter but stockier than Kip suggests.

Unlike the boy who corrected Kip's fists, this man looks quite capable of causing harm if he wanted to. The large quantity of scars on his arms show evidence of the many battles that he obviously won, or at the least survived—which is a win in its own right.

"It's okay. I have this. It never leaves my..." Kip taps his side only to feel nothing there. He quickly looks down and realizes that his little belt dagger is missing. It must have fallen off at some point during all the commotion.

A ruckus erupts among everyone as to what weapon Kip should take for protection. They're boasting about their own gear being "legendary" or "magical." One person professed that their clawed gloves are "sharper than a dragon's tooth." Their voices quickly escalate, completely drowning out the booming sounds that are increasing from the outside danger.

All Kip wanted to do was blend in, but somehow it has inexplicitly become all about him. The whole castle is filled with people, some of them must be more inept than him, surely. But for some reason, he is getting the brunt of it—all of it.

"Everyone, stop! Can we all focus on the people who need help out there?" Kip yells, finding his voice, though it does crack like an adolescent going through puberty.

"He's right," Taarl says. "We need to move this along before there isn't anyone left to save out there."

Slowly, other unarmed, or otherwise ill-equipped, people find their way out of the crowd, approach the pile, and start to grab some gear themselves. This makes Kip feel slightly better. He wasn't the only one who didn't prepare for battle. They were here the whole time. Only, they were much better at hiding in the back than he was.

One man picks up a sword and notices that it is a fake—obviously part of someone's costume. A couple of onlookers fail at hiding their laughter, making it obvious who donated that piece of junk.

The stress leaves Kip's shoulders as he blows out all the air out of his lungs. No one seems to be noticing him anymore, and his nervous tic is at bay...for now. "Feast or famine," Kip says under his breath. He looks down at the boots, which are still next to him. Not wanting to cause a riot, he slips into them one foot at a time. They're a couple sizes too big, but they will do nicely.

Before he can sneak off into the background again, he feels a firm hand on his shoulder. It causes him to jump almost a foot off the ground.

"Take this. It is the only thing you'll need," the bearded man says, removing his steel helm and plopping it on Kip's smaller head.

"I don't think..."

"If you get into trouble—and you will—just hide with all the children. Don't get in our way. You hear me?"

"Yes...sir." Kip looks to the floor, feeling less than nothing.

"I mean it. If you get within my reach, I won't hesitate in removing you from this world and taking back my hat."

Kip knows he is telling the truth, and that's what hurts the most.

Day One, 9:37 am: The Guard

While finishing the final touches for setting up his booth, Kip catches a glimpse of a hooded figure brushing by his table. Instantly he knows that the culprit swiped his box of paper vouchers right from under his nose. Without those notes, Kip will not be able to trade any wares at this moneyless event. They are as good as gold and as good as gone.

"Hey! There's a—you know—a...thief!" Kip hesitantly says, not sure of exactly what to do in this situation. He thought that the invention of the bartering system was supposed to prevent the event from theft. The doors are not even open to the public yet. Never did he think that another merchant or event staff would be so bold as to commit the crime against him.

Grabbing his face in utter shock, Kip is paralyzed momentarily as he watches the back of the thief as he runs away with his life savings in voucher notes. He only purchased that many notes to opt in to the bulk conversion rate the festival committee was promoting. This was going to be his final event, or so he hoped.

Instead of taking action, he is inundated

with questions in his mind. *What if they don't refund me the full amount? This would mean that my whole week would be a total bust—I don't even have enough money for food for the long trek home.*

This is catastrophic, and the ramifications are endless. His mind is quickly going through them all. Each new possibility crunches his face ever so slightly, as if it is going to compact into itself.

"That's not for decoration, is it?" Sarl, the vendor next to him, asks, pointing to the dagger on Kip's hip.

That is a very interesting question indeed. For Kip is in a transitional period at the moment—hero or coward? Those lines never used to be so blurred. He once knew who he was and what he wanted to be. It was fate that caused him to question everything he was, shattering the ignorance that kept him pure for so long.

"Well, I..." Kip wants to be reactionary and let his actions speak for him, but it is his dreadful mind that keeps him constrained and won't let him. Sure, when he has time to mull over a problem and all the possible outcomes, he manages to come up with a reasonable solution—such as his idea to come to this event year after year. In a pinch, however, he just sits there frozen with uncertainty.

"He's getting away," Sarl cries out mockingly, utterly confused by why his neighbor isn't doing something, anything.

Kip grips on to his weapon tightly. His hand is shaky against the hilt. Sweat drips down his face as he takes aim. Sure, he's never thrown a weapon like this before, but how hard can it be?

What if I miss? What if I hit someone else. His eyes scan back and forth looking for small children that might dart in the way of his throw. *I can do this. People throw stuff all the time. I just have to focus and think good thoughts.* With an outstretched arm, and holding the blade entirely the wrong way, he is ready to take his shot at greatness.

Before he can leap on the opportunity to prove to himself that he isn't useless, a castle guard tackles the thief with ease...and without hesitation.

"Phew." Kip lets his shoulders sink. If he had thrown the blade, he most likely would have hit the guard. He got lucky this time, and luck isn't something to take for granted because—like most good things—once it runs out, the darkness takes over.

"Do you always let other people fight your battles for you, kid?" Sarl asks.

"It's Kip. Not kid."

"I know. That's what I said."

"No, you didn't," Kip mouths to himself without actually saying the words.

"See that move he's doing? He could snap his arm if he wanted to. It's quite easy, really," Sarl says, already moving on to marveling at the strength and skill of the guard. "I used to work patrol, but we never had armor like that. But then again, we were only guarding water, not a whole castle."

After binding the thief's hands and legs together, the guard pats his hands together twice as if to say, "All done."

Holding the stolen vouchers in one hand, the guard approaches Kip and Sarl who are acting like wallflowers. "Either of you Kip, with Seeds and Weeds?" the guard asks with a serious tone in his voice. He is all business.

Reluctantly, Kip starts to hold up a finger, but Sarl swats it down without even a glance back to him.

"How much is there?" Sarl asks, with a sly grin.

"Enough to start a small armory," the guard

responds, showing where his mind is at.

"Then that's me." Sarl blurts out a laugh.

"No, it's me! I mean...those are mine."

The guard slowly sizes Kip up and down. "No wonder he robbed you."

"Excuse me?"

Sarl and the guard share a chuckle and butt elbows.

There is something about Kip's appearance that is somehow humorous to them, though Kip doesn't understand why they're mocking him so.

"The real question is, why *wouldn't* you rob him? I mean if I only knew he had a small fortune instead of those useless plants, I would have cleaned him out and been halfway to Drakus by now." Sarl adds fire to the burning unpleasantries.

"Stop messing around, you guys," Kip says, reaching for the box of procured notes. A slight twitch comes to his eye.

The guard snaps back his arm, holding the vouchers slightly out of reach. "Are you sure you want these back?"

"Come on. Yes, of course, I do," Kip whines. This whole ordeal is starting to draw a small crowd of people to his booth. Under normal circumstances, he would leap at an opportunity to sell to bored vendors. However, he doesn't like being humiliated in order to get their attention.

"I can keep them for him and issue an allowance," Sarl tells the guard.

"Here you go," the guard says, dropping the box on Kip's table.

Quickly, Kip opens it up. He counts the paper sleeves, making sure everything is accounted for. The vouchers are there, but something else isn't. "Did you see anything else in there?"

"I didn't take anything, if that's what you're implying," the guard says, looking serious again.

"Not vouchers. My medicine was in here."

"I didn't see nothing like that," the guard says. "Hey, stop that!" The guard notices his hog-tied thief trying to hop away in the distance, and he rushes over to him.

"Medicine, huh? It all makes sense. I thought you seemed a little crazy," Sarl comments.

"It's not that sort of thing," Kip says through gritted teeth.

Up until now, Kip wasn't sure if he liked or

hated his neighbor. Now it is clear...he hates him with all of his being.

This is, of course, naive behavior, only he doesn't know it yet...

Day Three, 3:33 am: Escape

Outside the inner gatehouse, as they near the drawbridge, Kip's legs burn hot with the friction from being dragged moments ago.

There is nothing he can do except wait for the crowd to disperse so that he can return to the good fight. Anxiety begins to build within him. "Come on, come on. Hurry up already."

This battle has created a break in the assault, and an opportunity for the innocents to flee towards the front of the castle. Somehow the gate is operational, and the drawbridge is down. This is the only exit large enough to facilitate an evacuation of this caliber. Directing the traffic, Kip waves his hands until the last of the crowd is on their way to the exit. "Get out while you still can. Let's go."

Smiling faces and hopeful eyes greet him as he takes charge in the evacuation. Things are looking up for them. Escape might be the only reasonable option for everyone at this point.

A man wearing a green tunic with tassels on the fringe grabs Kip's forearm. "Hey, come with us, friend." He has kind eyes and a big square-jawed smile.

With a shake of his head, Kip says, "No, I'm okay. You go."

"Come on. Freedom is right over there. Can't you smell it?" The man closes his eyes and breathes in deep.

"I wish I could, but I have things I need to attend to first."

"All right, friend. You hold things down here, and I'll get help."

"It's a deal." Kip gives the man a fraudulent smile. He wants to join them, but he can't just abandon all of his responsibilities. Not now. Not after he has seen so much. This is bigger than him—the biggest thing that has ever happened to him—and he must see it through.

Once the last stragglers are on their way, Kip doesn't know what to do with himself.

A bright wave of force explodes from the direction of the drawbridge.

"What was that?" He wonders if they got out in time, or if he has led them all to their sudden doom...

Tripping over himself, Kip runs to the front

of the castle for clarification.

Among the fleeing crowd, torch light is sparkling off of metal armor. It shines as a beacon of salvation.

Help has arrived. Judging by the regalia, they must be castle guards. Trained and outfitted for this sort of unrest, their suits look identical—even though most of their tabards are torn to shreds or charred beyond recognition. Kip's knows that it's unheard of to see a group of people dressed similarly without being hired, in some form or another.

In every region, new styles and improvements are made in armor and weaponry nearly each fortnight. You could say they're in a smiting renaissance, in a sense. Kusan Marbe is partially to blame for this trend. His steel-working designs have revolutionized both the aesthetic appeal and practical efficiency in the field. If you manage to get yourself on a Kusan, you keep it no matter if it's last season's design.

Eventually though, talent overcomes gear in the broader scheme of things. It might be superstition or a bond between a warrior and their weapon after a kill is made, but you can always tell how seasoned a warrior is by the condition and age of their equipment. This reasoning is why Kip believes that they are guards—they are far too uniformly dressed.

Unless...a dark thought forms inside his exhausted mind. *What if they're some of the usurpers?* Only a large force such as an army could fell such a castle of this size and stature.

When it comes to fight or flight, the latter seems like the most sensible plan. Kip quickly looks back and forth for an exit route, looking for a chance to flee, like a burning man towards a fountain.

As quickly as his mind switched sides, it happens again upon seeing one of the armored men helping a kid dressed in a character costume out of some rubble. They have to be guards, he now knows for certain—no sieging army would care about the young of their enemies—no matter how great of a costume they had on.

Unless they're slavers. Capturing children is not something that Kip is going to stand for.

He wants to rise up to them and liberate the child, but he just can't. He feels like a unbroken horse fearing the corrective sting of his master's whip.

Although Kip has never actually met a living, breathing slaver, he can't imagine them being this well-organized, with coordinated armor and such.

Getting a better look at an armored man's face—clean-shaven, mild-mannered—he decides that anyone in the slave game must show their inner cruelty, through missing teeth or otherwise. Stereotype or not, he believes in this one hundred percent.

This was a misunderstanding and another case of his imagination getting away from him. It is clear now that they really are helping the kid out.

If they're not our attackers, who or what is? This thought brings a nervous feeling to his stomach. It is already the second day of destruction, and though Kip has been a witness to many terrible things, never has he actually seen the source of it.

Could they be invisible? He has heard the stories of some people so ugly, so vile, and so hideous that they soon became invisible to everyone around them—never to be pointed or laughed at again. They are known as the night stalkers. Fairytales are written about these folks—about how they rape, murder, and steal from their sleeping victims, but only to those who have done them harm.

Kip is always kind and overly polite, so he doesn't have to worry. But still, worry he does. Night stalkers are one of his most feared tales, and even though it is more likely an urban legend, he doesn't take any chances when it comes to paranoia.

With a quick turn of his head, he starts to hear sounds that aren't there, people that aren't attacking him.

No, that can't be. I'm not thinking straight again. But then he hears it again, the sound of combatants clashing swords and carving into meat.

Once the thought enters his mind, there is no stopping it. He vividly imagines a person getting cut down. Each detail rich and gory, all the way down to the horrid expression of the fallen corpse. It doesn't matter if it isn't happening; it feels real, and his disgust is very much there, fiction or not.

What I need is sleep. He tries to get a grip on what is real and what his mind is fabricating.

Fast and hard, grotesque images of all the people he has seen murdered over the past few days haunt him. Over and over they come, pounding against his sanity. It isn't the horrible expressions of pain that are painted on their faces; it's the sorrow hidden behind their eyes that gets to him. Real, deep anguish. The kind you cannot shake off or erase from your thoughts.

Falling to his knees, Kip lets out a series of screams. It is all he can do to drown out the voices acting as ingredients to the poison soup he is feeding his overactive mind.

Feeling the cold steel of a gauntlet on his shoulder, Kip turns silent and still, shaking like a madman.

Had they found him? Is this the end of the travesty in the never-ending day of destruction? He doesn't know what to believe anymore.

As his eyes adjust to the torch light, the figure touching him comes into view. It's a castle guard.

"Come with us. We're trying to get everyone out of here," the guard says with compassion and care in his eyes.

Hope refills Kip, like a frostbitten hunter curling up to a warm hearth.

With a loud crack, a nearby flagpole snaps.

Before Kip realizes where the sound is even coming from, the guard is quick on his feet, running towards the sound, making his own racket with each refined movement.

Leaping through the air while wearing a full set of standard-issue steel armor, the guard manages to knock a nearby elderly man out of harm's way right before the flagpole comes crashing down. It is much bigger on the ground than it looked when it was three stories up. If it wasn't for the guard's quick reaction time, the man surely would have been crushed by the massive pole.

The elderly man has a couple scrapes and bruises, but he is otherwise fine from the incident.

Kip recognizes this hero. It's none other than the guard that made him feel foolish two days ago over those damn coin vouchers. Not just anyone can do something like that. He is special, one of the good ones. Never mind how he made Kip feel before. All is forgiven with this act. The discontentment he had towards the guard is now replaced by honor and a level of celebrity he bestows upon him.

"Should I say something? Nah. He won't even remember me. And besides, would I want him to?" Kip says to himself just under his breath, his jittering fingers telling more of the story.

Even though he did nothing, Kip feels a pang of exhaustion from the whole incident. Maybe it's the aftermath of all the adrenaline leaving his body. He needs a minute to recover.

Taking a beat, Kip observes the guards at their tasks. It appears as though they're ushering people to escape out of the castle some other way.

He catches sight of the heroic guard assisting the elderly man he just saved. From Kip's vantage point, it is unclear where they're going or what they're doing. It is all somewhere just outside of his line of sight. With the curiosity of a cat, he follows their path.

Once there, there don't seem to be any people left to observe. Kip dusts himself off to take a closer look.

A loud rumbling sound excites the air around him, followed by a plume of dust and debris.

"What is it now?" After the cloud settles, he searches for the guards, the people...anything. Only, he finds that no one is there. Where could they have all gone to?

The castle's drawbridge is clamped shut like the mighty jaws of a dragon. It must have been the source of the loud noise. Could they have opened it? Did he miss his only opportunity to leave? Now that the moment has passed, he regrets not leaving when he had the chance.

Not far from the massive door is an alcove housing an impressive mechanism that operates the bridge. Kip tries to turn the crank that holds the chain at bay, although he is only one man—one who isn't particularly strong to begin with. With all his might, he tries and tries, but it just won't budge, not even a little bit. It's no use. He cannot finish the task that the mighty guards were embarking on.

"People must have escaped. Where else would they be if they hadn't?"

Next to the crank, Kip notices a grappling hook void of a rope set. Lucky for Kip, he has a rope without a hook to accompany it. This must be fate, he knows.

When all seems to be lost, fortune finds him yet again. The moat isn't particularly wide, and even he can make the throw to the other side, he hopes. And now Kip is optimistic again. He can leave and get help, get someone else to come and put an end to this surreal madness—someone stronger, someone faster, someone...else.

Nothing can stop his fingers from swiftly

entangling his own supply of rope to the grappling hook that chance has blessed him with. One of the hook's points bores a hole into his shirt—scraping his flesh. Before the pain has a chance to set in, he takes a bite of his medicine root.

"I have to be much more careful. Relax." He gets back to his task. This time he takes his time. After giving the rope a mighty tug, the knot holds, and it feels right to him.

Everything is ready. He takes in a long, deep breath, trying to calm his nerves before making this life-or-death feat of physical prowess. This is his ticket out of here. A slight smile tries to creep onto his dirt-riddled face, but he pushes back the feeling.

"You are on the cusp of freedom. This is all going to be over soon," he assures himself. With those words of encouragement still resonating inside his ears, he swings the rope and deadly points around his head, gaining momentum with every revolution.

Faster and faster it goes. He doesn't know when to stop. One false move can lead to catastrophe...or worse, death.

When do I let it loose? This is much harder than it looks. Not that he has ever seen anyone use the thing, though the overall concept is generally understood by most.

Failure happens mostly when he tries too hard. But that is okay, because when he falls down, he always gets up again and again. Kip closes his eyes. He feels the whirlwind of air above him at every turn. He imagines himself taking flight inside it—free, like a bird.

Then, without rhyme or reason, he blindly releases his grip on the rope, letting it soar through the air. It is flying through the air.

"The rope!" His eyes flash open the moment he realizes that he wasn't supposed to let go of the rope completely, or else the end might go who knows where.

Launching on his stomach towards the unraveling rope, his hands burn hot from all the friction. He manages to get a grip on it with both hands, jolting him forward into the edge of the castle wall. If one stone comes loose, he is going over the edge for sure. So far, it is holding strong.

He takes solace in seeing that the grapple is heading in the correct direction, over the moat, and not in the direction of the oil containers to his right, the very ones that are used to burn people scaling the walls. Even though they're not heated up at the moment, getting doused in oil isn't his idea of a good time.

Hearing the sound of the hook colliding with something over the ravine, he tugs against it. He's imagining himself a fisherman catching a fish and pulling the hook through its mouth. Only, this is the biggest catch he has ever caught—freedom. The grappling hook is in fact caught on something. The rope goes taught. He has done it. Despite himself, it really worked.

Before tying his end of the rope on to a metal ring, he looks down at his hands. They are raw and blood red with rope burn. Somehow he didn't feel a thing other than a slight tingle. He knows that if he had felt that kind of burning pain, he wouldn't have been able to grip the rope and suffer through it. Pain has a way of controlling him, making him do things against his own heart, but not today.

Kip glances over the edge of the wall to the ravine below. Somehow he doesn't expect to see so many corpses at the bottom. Either they fell off the bridge or leapt to their death into the dry moat. He is unsure of which. He can barely see the grass that grows beneath all the fallen corpses.

"That is a lot of people. That didn't just

happen, did it?"

Circling the skies, he notices some night buzzards, which tells him otherwise. There is no way those birds could have come this fast.

Through curious eyes, Kip scours through the bodies on the bottom of the moat, looking for the guard that helped him twice. It is too dark and much too far to know for certain. If it wasn't for two fallen torches, he wouldn't be able to see a thing.

"I should've stopped that thief myself." Kip says to the wind, wishing that time would reverse and make him into the person he once was. Maybe then he might also be the type of person to stop whatever is hurting all these good people.

"You hear me? I would take it all back if I could. Let me do it. Let me be the one to die in glory, not these brave people!"

He looks up, taking in the black skies. Pure and clean, and without visions of harm. "I could have been among them."

Reluctantly Kip glances back down at what is left behind—armor, weapons, corpses. Dead is dead, but somehow the notion that they all met their end a day, or even hours earlier, gives Kip some level of comfort.

He imagines the sound of the dead laughing at him and his cowardice. Through hollow lips, they're taunting him about his failures in saving them.

"I have a family waiting for me at home."

"You didn't try hard enough."

"You don't even remember, do you?"

"And you call yourself a hero."

"All you care about is saving yourself."

"No, it's not like that," Kip says. His eyes dart around sharply, trying not to focus on all the pain piled up at the bottom of the moat.

"I didn't do this. It's not my fault." He feels the sense that the line between his madness and sanity is growing thinner by the second.

Then, off in the distance, he sees a couple of figures on the other side of the moat. That is the real source of the laughter. Instantly his sanity is restored.

"Someone escaped. That means that they can get help." Even now, Kip tries to look at the bright side of the situation.

It could have been easy for a few guards to flee and leave the civilians to fend for themselves, though they kept to their oath and duty and brought people less than themselves.

When Kip was scared out of his wits, the

guards took up arms and had enough courage to face the danger head-on. That is true heroism—to go up against unspeakable odds, no matter the cost.

With new-found courage, he ties the rope off.

"Those survivors will seek help, and now they can use my rope to get back in. I am not going to run away, not after everything I've been through. It is my turn to step it up and hold down the fort." Kip is ready to do something.

Floating through the air is a burnt flag of the once great stronghold, a perfect metaphor to what his life has become—lost and hurt, but not quite done yet.

Liquid Life

"Oh, the unspeakable event has caused most people to flee or go into hiding. Only the Maker knows what has happened to the heroic ones. The only evidence I saw was that they never came back with words of glory. Maybe they are together again in the promised lands.

"What was supposed to be a time of happiness, heartfelt art, good food, and great friends has turned a course to the wicked, and it is only getting worse with each passing moment. Looking over at the blackened sky, I cannot help but wonder how many moments we have left in us.

"It's a devastating time, with no end in sight. Only death, destruction, and repentance remain.

"People think I am a goodly person. I give

"

my abundance to charity, I'm very punctual, and I never cut the line at suppertime. Somehow all the rules have changed. Everyone is equal under the eyes of the end-bringer.

"I always used to pray to a greater power. Dear me, now that I've seen such power, there is nothing great about it. Judgment is upon us, and it takes no prisoners. It's too late for me and absolutions. In a place full of good intentions, I was caught in the middle of a spider's den. I took a wrong turn and stood my ground—face-to-face with the Maker himself. I never had a chance, but I had to try with all my being. That is what a younger me would have wanted anyway. Only, I had no fighting prowess, no weapon to strike with. That mattered not. It was the only reasonable option; praying would solve nothing—not this time. Alas, I did what I had to. What would you have done if I were you?" -*Maggie the Widow, age 81.*

Day One, 8:04 am: Registration

With an extra spring in his step, Kip makes his way to his pop-up booth. Like a pack horse, he has bags on his bag, crates and materials stacked between his arms. They are so high in fact that he has to tilt his head slightly just to see through his baggage. His small muscles struggle with the freshly painted signs, banners, table wrappings, handout flyers, and everything else he has made for the occasion.

Setup and teardown are physically the hardest part of the harvest. Emotionally, making sales and talking to people are much worse. His quest is well worth stepping out of his comfort zone for a couple of days and the long excursion south.

The crisp chill of the harvest fills Kip with a warmth of achievement. A task he never thought was possible to complete in his lifetime was nearly fulfilled. Not once before has he had faith in himself to execute such an ordeal, but here he is, living proof of such a victory.

He can't believe that almost three years have passed since he first met the half-breed who turned his life upside down. What Kip once thought of as profit is now considered pocket change compared to what he is going to outlay during this week-long festival.

The castle gates are closed off to the large sea of attendees that is rushing in more quickly than a rising tide. From here, Kip hears the loud cheers and howling sounds. It's clear that everyone is chomping at the bit to kick off the festivities. Inside, the vendors and participants are preparing for the opening of the flood gates.

Kip manages to reach the registration table before his arms fall off completely. "I'm Kip, in the bartering sector," he says to the elderly woman who has more wrinkles than the average prune.

"You can put that down, if you like," she says, noticing his struggle.

"Thanks." With a loud thud and a deep sigh of relief, he drops his gear, then shakes out his arms. They are floppy like overly cooked noodles.

The woman rummages through a stack of papers, looking to make sure his dues are paid in full. "Kip, you say?"

The young human catches himself looking at her misshapen bosom which is crammed into a corset seemingly three sizes too small for her large frame. Kip can't help but notice the extra flesh contorting and popping out in an unnatural sort of way. He isn't trying to be a heel or a cad at all. It's just nearly impossible for him to ignore them—sticking out like the focal point of the whole outfit.

"A man stares like that, he should have to

pay for the view," the woman says to him, holding out a badge and lanyard.

"I didn't mean to. I..." Kip feels horrible. She has mistakenly pegged him as some kind of creep. He wasn't looking at her in a lustful way; it was from a place of intrigue—as to where all that flesh was coming from and where it was going. Kip rifles through his coin purse and pulls out a shiny silver shilling. *Is this too much or too little,* he wonders.

"I'm only fooling with ya. I ain't no girl for hire." she says with a jack-o'-lantern smile.

Kip's gaze becomes blinkless, as he uses every ounce of constraint to not let his eyes meet her chest again. It is like an awkward staring contest where he is playing against his own self-respect...and losing.

"I meant no disrespect. You have to believe me. I'm not that kind of man."

"These be out here for lookin' and starting conversations," she admits, proudly brushing the hair away from her neckline.

With his eyes locked on hers, he rifles through his tote, looking for something to calm this whole situation and restore his honor among the women folk of these parts. If anything, he doesn't want to start to get a bad reputation, especially not on the first day. "Here it is. I have this letter…" Kip extends his hand out to the mistress of the fair.

Thinking this piece of paper has something to do with business, the woman takes the parchment from his jittery hand.

"To whom it may concern: In most recent years, though misunderstood, Kip has proven to be a gentleman and an utterly trustworthy companion and compatriot. In many…" The woman's face turns sour and confused as she reads the letter aloud. "What in the open grave is this?"

"A letter of recommendation, from a *real*, nice girl…"

"Get the hell out of here before I call the guards."

"What did I do wrong?"

"Get gone!"

Flustered, Kip grabs his badge and letter as quickly as possible, but stacking all of his other things is a little harder to do in a flash. With all his mounds of stuff in his hands teetering from making a huge mess, he makes his way towards his table two districts away. Confrontation isn't his forte, nor is spending a night in a jail cell for harassment.

If this is a taste of things to come in the up-coming week, Kip is due for a rude awakening.

Day Three, 7:03 am: Broken Leg

Running for his life from the horrid thing behind him, Kip trips over some hidden object in his path. A piece of the castle wall has shifted and now sticks out like an intentional foot in a childhood prank.

Tumbling to the ground and over himself a couple times, he slams into a pillar. It is a hard hit, the kind that requires a moment to recover from. Except, he finds that he is not the only victim of this unintentional trap. Next to him is the woman he recognizes from the registration table, boobs and all.

"Hey, are you okay?" Kip asks, ignoring the bump on his head and newly acquired head-ache.

She is barely conscious and rolls her neck over to him. "What?"

As he shifts closer to her, he notices that her leg bone is sticking out of her leggings in a con-torted sort of way. It would appear that she has fared far worse than he has in the accident.

"I said, are you okay?" Kip repeats himself,

softer this time.

"I can't walk." She slurs her words, as if intoxicated with pain, looking at him lazily, with one eye closed.

Kip tries to assist her up, though without her help, nothing he can do will yield him enough leverage to bring her to her feet. He's just not strong enough.

The horrible barking sound that was chasing him starts to catch up to them once again.

"We have to go," he keeps repeating to the woman.

The sounds of death gets louder as it echoes throughout the halls. Followed by unnatural screams, which hurt their ears.

Upon hearing the sounds for herself, a flash of life returns to her tired eyes, and she tries to stand.

Kip gets underneath her and uses his whole body to prop her up on one leg. It is working. Together they are doing it.

Out in the open sky, an enigmatic cloud of energy appears. It moves around like a hunter, fast and deadly. Before anything can be done, a bolt of energy touches the woman and liquefies her instantly.

Her bodily contents dissolve everywhere,

across the hallway, the ground, and most unfortunately, all over Kip.

He stands there speechless, afeard of taking in even a single breath. This can't be real, but somehow it is. Something has the power to destroy so instantaneously, and it just used it with malice aforethought.

There is nothing left of her but a damp pile of her belongings. Resting on her once ill-fitting corset is a sun-embroidered coin purse.

Out of nowhere, a man runs in and steals the money pouch from her pile of gore. Another bolt of energy takes him in the same manner as the woman, before Kip can do a thing about it. Another wave of red slashes across the castle wall, but this time Kip is too far away to get struck by it.

Next to her pile is the thief's much larger pile of loot, which he most likely plundered.

Kip waits for his turn to die, though it doesn't come, not yet...

Day Four, 11:01 am: Remorse

Curled up in the fetal position, Kip reflects on the past as tears stream down his face—washing away the woman's dried blood that once drenched him. Despondency nearly consumes him completely.

She wasn't the greatest to him, but she also wasn't that bad to him, either. In any case, no one deserves what happened to her.

A couple of days ago, they had spoken and shared a moment...but moments never last forever, nor do people, their insides, or anything else, for that matter.

How could he wipe away the grotesque fluid of death off his brow? She was someone once, and now this is all that is left of her, something to be discarded like some sort of filth. To clean himself off means to wipe her out of existence. As horrible as the goo makes him feel, nothing is worse than nothingness.

Why couldn't he have been hit by the bolt instead, and his leftovers staining her face and clothes. In some ways, dying instantly is far better than the torture of waiting for your own demise.

The more he thinks about the poor woman and everyone else he has seen die, the faster his tears come. Unless he wants to die from dehydration, action is his only recourse.

He hears the sound of a woman's torment in the far-off distance. Part of him wonders if he knows who she is. After days of trauma, all pain sounds the same. He can't help anyone; he is only going to make matters worse. They are better off without him, he knows.

This brings him deeper into the anguish of this gory incident. "I have to do it. This is too much."

A chorus of child-like hushes fills the small chamber, while little fingers press over pursed lips call out to silence him.

Kip's trembling hand holds some salm root. He is tempted to ingest its milky liquid and end all of his suffering in one fell swoop. While bringing it up to his lips, he is a moment away from nothingness, yet he refrains. A memory invades him in a moment of clarity...

Taking Back the Night

"In the vast ocean of pain, each wave moves aimlessly—existing only to fill space. Courage rises to the top like oil, acting as a shield for the weak to hide under its glorious sheen. I was once that glimmering piece of hope.

"I am powerful, but will it be enough? Was there ever a chance for it to be? I pleaded with the night. I gave up my honor, putting my self-respect on the line. I tried to bargain with the devil for salvation, and it devoured my shame with beautiful magic.

"As it stole my soul, I felt that I was part of something bigger now, something everlasting. This was what it must feel like to be a god—to take without permission, to harm without guilt...to destroy. This was hell. With every bit I had left, I resisted.

"If you can hear me—what is left of me—send my love to humanity and remind it that I'm sorry, so very sorry. I have failed. We all failed." *-Royal Knight, age unknown.*

Day Two, 9:39 pm: The Plan is Forming

The brilliantly bright attacks vine through the air every couple of seconds. They're keeping the adventurers from adventuring outside. Nothing can compete with a power like that. It goes through armor and shields without care or reason.

The painful groans from beyond the stone walls keep everyone on edge. There's nothing they can do for them now. Taking refuge is the only reasonable answer.

Kip tries to convince himself that people are just acting scared out there; it can't be half as bad as it sounds from inside here. His mind is playing the part of a pessimist as a coping mechanism.

Everyone is ready for battle, armed with traditional weapons, alongside some make-shift costume pieces adapted for practical uses. One fighter has driven a couple of decorative claws through the cracks in his wooden shield, turning it into a blocking weapon.

These are the best and the bravest around. Ready to take up arms and put an end to whatever it is that is out there.

"As far as we know, it is some sort of lightning attack. It shocks, stuns, and can even kill you instantly," Taarl admits.

"Is there really no way to block it?" a young man asks.

"Unfortunately, it's like a spider's web, except if you're within twenty feet of it, you're dinner," Taarl continues grimly.

"That isn't what I experienced. I came out of the art show, and there was something different in the sky. Like some sort of pulse attack," a man with skull-bone armor interjects.

"That's where we're heading now. Why did you leave, coward?" asks a tall man who has fashioned a guillotine into an axe head.

"Do you want to say that again to my face?" the skull-armored man threatens.

The bearded man who gave Kip his steel helm abruptly stands, ready for an all-out fight to break out. In fact, he looks excited for just that. "I ran towards the foe, not away."

"If you were not running away, how did you

end up here?" Kip asks innocently.

"I cannot kill effectively without this!" the bone-armored man says, unsheathing his great sword, which has a hilt made out of a crocodile skull.

Two people have to duck to avoid getting hit by the monstrosity that is his weapon. If anything, it is impressively large.

Looking up, Kip goes over the map in his head that he has of the castle. On the other side of the vendors is where the travelers lodging is located. Kip knows that the bone-armored man must have had to return there to get equipped for battle. After a beat of calculations, the man's story checks out.

"That thing isn't any match for my saber," a voice chimes in.

"You're all strong; we get it. Let him continue," Taarl interjects.

"If what you're saying is true, then...what does this mean?" Kip blurts out without thinking.

"I'll tell you what it means. There are multiple foes," the bone-armored man concludes.

"Maybe even a whole army," a young man suggests.

"I agree. It sounds like it's coming from

everywhere. That's the only explanation," the bone-armored man says with a nod.

"No one man could kill so effectively, that's for sure," Taarl says.

"Or woman," Kip says, looking at a female warrior, trying to make her feel comfortable.

She rolls her eyes at Kip in disgust. "It has pure power," she adds.

"It doesn't matter how many there are. I will kill them all myself," the bone-armored man declares, placing his bone-handled great sword over his shoulder.

"Let's not rush into this until we find out what we're dealing with," a bowman says, outstretching a calming hand.

"I have a plan," says a man covered head to toe in tarnished armor, his voice muffled from inside his suit. He holds a large silver lance, which scrapes the ceiling as he takes the center of the room.

Where did that guy come from. Kip most assuredly would have noticed someone head to toe covered in platemail armor before.

"I know you. You're just a stage combatant. What are you going to do?" an axe-wielding man insults the newcomer.

"I may be a performer, but I am also well

trained. True, the battles I fight are fake, but our weapons are very much real. As opposed to some of the junk you guys are reduced to using."

"I would rather take my chances alone out there than follow some actor," the axe man says, affirming his previous statement.

"Let him talk. I want to hear this," Kip says, as he is out of any ideas of his own to add to the mix.

"Oh, be quiet, you," the female Kip stood up for moments ago admonishes.

"If anyone else has any other ideas, speak now. If not, I am willing to hear him out, false knight or not," Taarl says, standing in front of the performer.

There are a couple soft murmurs, but no one takes the center stage.

"Do tell. I'm open to anything at this point," someone from the crowd speaks up.

"Alright then," Taarl says, with a bow towards the false knight.

"This is what I got. I will take care of that storm. While some of you take care of all the wounded out there," the false knight says casually.

"And the rest of us?" Taarl is quick to ask.

"You charge in and slay those cunt bastards."

His vulgarity really hits home and is met with cheers and shouts. Everyone is getting fired up.

"Wait, how? Excuse me," Kip asks waving his arms.

"Be quiet. Everyone settle down. Let him speak," Taarl calms the crowd.

The room goes quiet, but everyone's eagerness for blood is still visible on their faces.

"Thank you. Um, how are you going to take care of the threat exactly?" Kip asks earnestly.

"Just stand back and get ready." The false knight slowly walks towards the exit, dragging a chain that is attached to his lance.

"But...how?" Kip looks back and forth for answers. Except no one else seems to care about his tactics, only that he is willing to do something, and something is better than nothing in this case.

"My fans await, and I will give them the greatest fucking performance of my life," the false knight shouts as he charges onward to the outside brimming with death.

Kip wonders how many years this knight has played the part of the hero. Only now, he is no longer pretending. He is acting out the part to perfection.

Day Four, 12:13 pm: Childhood Memories

Hiding for the last couple hours with the children makes Kip feel equally small and insignificant. He is not worth living, not worth the air he is stealing. He can't bear to look at the disappointment in their little eyes any longer. All he can do is curl himself up as small as he feels and reflect on where it all went south.

He remembers being brave as a boy, a local hero that people used to boast about. His mother often called him her "little legend." However, most legends are embellished and not quite as grand as the stories that are told about them. And for Kip at least, this was proving to be true.

Remembering the past couple days and what he has gone through is an extremely difficult task indeed. Things are not quite adding up in his mind. One oddity is that he has never felt the sensation of pain so vividly. This heart-stopping pain holds him dead in his tracks. Even the thought of getting hurt further causes him a physical reaction. He isn't sure if he perhaps never got hurt like this before, or if he has somehow transformed into a weakling along the way. The pain in his leg and side radiates and lingers without an end in sight.

"I've been hurt like this before, right?" he whispers to himself. Drawing up an old memory, he recalls the first incident of conflict in his life...

Back in his homeland, young Kip and his best friend Trevors had previously called each other the worst insult they knew, "hog-huggers." This led to them not speaking to each other. Normally, they would have cool off for a week or so before being around each other again. However, this time they were both tasked with gathering wild onions from the pasture.

Tension was thick, with many more layers than the onions in their sacks. One false move could ignite their fiery tongues once more.

Neither one wanted to be there more than the other, but likewise, they didn't have anyone to complain to and vent out their frustrations.

A third person, Yulla, was also sentenced to gather the vegetables alongside them. She had braided hair and wore her father's signature large boots. "Why don't you two get over it already and talk to me. I'm bored," she said.

Kip looked up at Trevors with sincere eyes, hoping to find a resolution and put an end to their little feud.

Trevors, however, shot him a glare full of daggers at the very notion of a truce.

"This is silly, you guys."

Both boys turned their backs to one another in defiance.

"Okay, I will make you a deal. The first one to reach twenty onions will be my new best bud."

Not caring for her offer of friendship but rather a chance to bet against the other in competition, both boys rushed into action.

They were pulling onions so fast that they didn't notice nor care about how much they were damaging the vegetables in the process.

"Six," Trevors said, proudly.

"Oh, yeah? Eight!" Kip boasted.

"Oh my, that was easy. If you guys keep it up..."

"I counted wrong. I have eight too," Trevors lied, interrupting Yulia's praise.

One after another, they were neck and neck

in the task. Each declaration of quantity caused the other to gnash their teeth even more.

"I never knew you guys liked me so much," Yulia admitted coyly.

"Shush it, Yulia. We're busy...nineteen!" Trevors said.

"Twenty! I did it!" Kip said, out of breath.

It was then that Trevors threw his bag of broken onions on the ground in defeat.

"Hey, no need for that. Good sportsmanship is always key in any competition," Yulia said.

Kip jumped up and down, gloating his victory over Trevors. This was more about the argument than anything else. It was unspoken, but the winner of the onion race was instantly right in the previous night's conflict, and currently Kip was that winner.

"You cheated. You always cheat!" Trevors protested.

"No. *You* always cheat and blame other people as a distraction."

"Come on, stop it!" Yulia just wanted to make things better. "How about you're both my best buds?"

"Fine. As long as we all know who won, just like we know who cursed first," Kip said, ignoring the girl and her plea.

"You know what? You're acting exactly like you were last night, like a no-good hog-hugger!" Trevors said in a mocking, squeaky voice with a snort.

"Did you hear that? He started it again," Kip said, turning to Yulia.

"Don't get me involved," she said wisely.

Both boys got in each other's face, glaring and snarling. The tension rose from thick to as hard as a diamond, within a flash.

"You guys should kiss and make up," Yulia said, pushing Kip's back, knocking him into Trevors.

Kip's teeth bashed against the other boy's forehead, drawing a bloody bite mark.

Instantly a fight broke out between them. Trevors thought that Kip bit him on purpose and Kip thought that Trevors headbutted him. In either case, both were wrong and tussled on the floor.

Kip doesn't remember how that fight ended, but he had a black eye and more than a dozen scratches and bruises on his body. He never remembered it hurting or even getting hurt, only his mother treating his wounds, the way she always did.

Something about this memory doesn't add up for Kip, probably due to the missing information. So he searches his mind for another...

Smoke marked the sky where a fire had taken place. Following the trail in the sky, Kip ran with the intention of assisting the watering crew, though no one was at the scene. He was the first to arrive.

As far as he could tell, there was no sign of anyone being trapped inside of the stone home, but the straw roof was already ablaze. That didn't stop him from playing the part of the hero.

Without waiting for help to arrive, Kip bounded up to the front door and kicked at it until the hinges broke. Once he had gained access inside the building, he had to go inside.

Fearless, Kip rushed into the building, and the rest was a blur...

He remembers being the talk of the town, and that he saved two small children who were trapped inside, and that the house burnt completely out.

Years later, he and Trevors used to play inside the very site, and Kip even tried to reenact the event but couldn't.

If it weren't for him, those two kids never would have survived such a travesty. That is what the rumors always said, at least.

Why can't Kip remember how he did it? In the story, he was engulfed in flames and burned pretty badly. Every hair on his head was burnt off.

Like in the other story, his mother patched him up, and he made a complete recovery... Something wasn't right...with both stories.

Kip looks down at his blistered hands, *how did that happen?* Even his short term memory is now eluding him.

Kip starts piecing together a pattern. In each memory where he gets hurt he never remembers the part of injury, only the resolution and accolades that followed. He was considered a hero around his homelands. He was even called upon in moments of desperation and never disappointed. Or did he?

But that was then, and this is now. Something has drastically changed since those days.

"Someone has to do something, and if it's not me, then who?" Kip stands up, ready to make his move.

Day Two, 10:10 pm: Conductor

Without asking permission, or caring for his own well-being, the false knight plays his greatest role as a hero. All the bravest warriors follow in his valiant charge. Only Kip remains behind.

"What good can I do?" he asks himself, pacing back and forth.

So far, he has done nothing but mess things up. At every turn, his faith in himself has been shaken, to the point where he doesn't even trust himself anymore.

The battle sounds outside get louder and more intense with the arrival of the adventurers. A disarmed sword slides into the room with a couple fingers still gripping onto its hilt.

"I can't handle this anymore." Kip wants to lose himself to his own screams, but his pride is deafening. He feels like a parasite that is allergic to blood; the very thing he needs to survive is killing him from the inside.

Every part of his body aches with envy. He doesn't want to just join the false knight, he wants to be him—strong and admired, not whatever it is he is now.

Ever since he pinched himself and felt pain,

he hasn't been the same. He has been scared to death to even do anything. That small feeling is looming over him like a buzzard waiting for him to die. If a small pinch could hurt so very much, what does losing a couple fingers feel like? He desperately doesn't want to find out. The fear of pain is, in some cases, worse than experiencing the actual feeling.

"I have to do something with my life, or else it's all just wasted."

He briefly remembers the last time he felt this way. It was back when he was an adolescent. His friend Trevors said he would never amount to anything. That is why he called Trevors a hog-hugger and later lied about it.

But his friend wasn't wrong...not then and not now. Not about the hog-hugging part, but about not amounting to anything.

"It's time to put the pig to bed." No longer thinking of the consequences, Kip rushes in after the false knight and the rest of the mighty men and woman who are taking it upon themselves to put an end to this madness.

Entering the fray of the battleground, Kip's hair rises right off his head—reaching for the heavens. Electricity is in the air, but it doesn't hurt, it only makes him feel lighter somehow, like he is walking on a cloud.

Taarl looks over at Kip and yells, "We need more numbers."

Knowing exactly what Taarl is intimating, Kip quickly slinks back behind a pillar. *He needs more martyrs. I am not ready for anything like that.* The longer he debates with himself, the more the warriors are lost to the fight, but he knows he will just get in the way.

There is an overwhelmingly loud crackling sound of an electric surge. The bright light that has been creeping through the sky is now fixated on a single spot—the false knight, who is raising his lance high above his head triumphantly. His armor shakes and rattles as he convulses violently. Smoke pours out of the steel joints. A chain that is connected to his lance is wrapped around a nearby tower.

He is taking all the pain onto himself, allowing a break in the assault for the warriors to run through the barrier.

They are fired up and charging. The bearded man who gave Kip the steel helm, Taarl of the swampmen, the bone-armored man with his crocodile hilt great sword, the man with the guillotine axe, the woman with her cat-beast, and everyone else have their weapons drawn and are ready to slay.

This was the false knight's plan all along, to sacrifice himself for the greater good. He looks so glorious against the beautiful light that is killing him. Though tragic, Kip swears to erect a statue in his likeness to remember his deed. And that is a promise.

Things are Heating Up

"Friendship is giving compassion, time, attention, and support without ever wanting a return on your investment. Cherish those relationships because, once they're gone, you'll find that suddenly you're useless without them.

"Cleanse yourself of everything and you will become willing to accept anything. It's similar to how an empty heart is eager to accept love. To be selfless is to know thyself. To be vengeful is to know only fear. It takes a lot of anger and resentment to drive one's rage. Acceptance is both free and freeing of the spirit. It never gives in to the demon's demands. Everyone has a dark side hiding behind the light. One cannot be had without the other.

"I gave in to giving up. I toyed with a weapon

of my own creation. I couldn't live in a place so bland and bleak. I was faced with a game I no longer wanted to play. It was a choice of lesser evils, and I chose the path with a much sweeter end.

"While it may feel good to indulge in your wickedness, that hunger is never staved off for very long. Once you have a taste for it, your mind will ignore all reason and justify any or all crimes to get it. It's far better to be hungry for evil than full of pain." -*Chef Maximo, age 28.*

Day One, 6:20 am: High Hopes

Outside of the great marvel known as Castle Deep, Kip counts the piles of burlap sacks he had purchased for this year's festival. Though they're empty now, he dreams of returning in a week's time with them filled and stacked high atop his cart. The rough fabric reminds him of his friend Barne—the very person who's responsible for this whole journey in the first place. It seems like a lifetime ago when they first met in Scutter's Landing. Since that day, so much about himself has changed. Some for the better, others for the worse. On the surface, Kip's appearance might look no different, but the same couldn't be said about how he feels on the inside.

The wiry human came here for a specific purpose, one his destiny had to push the introvert into. What Kip lacks in brawn, he more than makes up for in persistence.

Once, meant as an insult, Kip was said to have a bit of a "girlish" frame. He doesn't let those types of comments affect him in the slightest, partially because he knows there is some truth to their intended insult, but mostly because he admires girls—women to be more exact. True, his body type doesn't yield him much stamina when it comes to fighting or manual labor tasks. So, instead, he thinks of schemes to get others more capable than himself to do his bidding...for a fair price, of course.

If something is out of your reach, pay someone taller to get it for you instead of falling off a chair. This is something his mother used to always say to him. When he was little, the meaning completely escaped him.

This upcoming event is where he hits pay dirt. In the past years, he acquired more items during the event than he had been able to scavenge on his own during all of the remaining months of the year combined. Anyone else would have given up on the daily grind and let the event grant them a year-long vacation. That would be the smart play, though his mission is that of moral obligation, one where he is caught chasing his own happiness, and anything short of complete diligence will not suffice.

You see, the young human has a talent, a very special one indeed—he must always do the right thing, no matter the cost. Sometimes he is a little slow in getting there, but he always comes through in the end. Justice and injustice are both ignored in this realm of lying low and keeping to yourself, but not if Kip has anything to say about it. Although, when he does, he doesn't have a loud or particularly command-ing voice, often whispers are what people listen to the hardest.

Scamming, disloyalty, and cutting corners are for those that don't want to put in the leg-work. To feel the weight of lifting everyone up on your shoulders and out of the mud is a bur-den Kip lives with but is never recognized for. He feels it alright, and it is that emotional pain that pushes him to work even harder.

Standing inside the looming structure's shadow, a smile flashes across his face. It's the festival's third year in existence, and attendance has more than quadrupled from the first incarnation. With each year that the show grows in size and attendees, Kip's sales go up equally. There is no reason to believe that this year is going to be any different. The first year was designated to just a few tables and displays in the courtyard. Rumor has it that this year has expanded into nearly every quarter of the castle. He has no reason to believe that every sack he brought is not going to be put to good use.

His excitement and optimism are peaking at the thought of possibly completing his quest and keeping true to his promise. This year could be the last, and who knows what the future has in store for him after that.

However, currently it is the unknown that has his aspirations held at bay. It is his life's goal to give life to those that had been unjustly slain by the old Lord. Doing right and erasing the wrongs is the greatest feeling Kip has ever experienced—a freeing sensation that lifts him above himself, much like how he imagines an eagle soaring across the sky feels.

The irony in this whole adventure is that in order to fix it, each year he must revisit the key location that was responsible for the near genocide of the feathered-folk. That was another world, one filled with darkness and revenge. This is the time of repair and rebirth, and Kip is a nurse aiding in the delivery of good things to come.

"It's easy to take. A much harder task is always in giving back. And for that, I accept your amends," Kip laments, looking at the towering structure casting its shade over him.

His statement has become part of his yearly ritual. It serves as a palate cleanser for the next chapter in his struggle. For him, hearing the words echo across the valley almost convinces him that someone is sharing in his views, even if it's just his own voice mirrored back to him. Deep down he knows this mantra is nothing more than a lie he continues to try and turn into truth. He feels that all words are nothing more than sounds that hold no particular power or meaning. If they did, lies would be extinct. It is actions that he believes are quite senior to words.

A large banner unrolls over the side of the castle's stone wall. With brightly painted colors and framed with freshly cut flowers, it reads, "Pleasure and play festival. All are welcome."

"Will you look at that. Fun awaits, doesn't it, boy?" Kip says to his mule-deer companion that has been pulling his cart for the entirety of the long journey.

The animal blows air out of its lips, almost as if it can understand him. True or not, it is always comforting for Kip to imagine it so.

"I know, it's quite boring in those stables all alone. Maybe this year, you might meet a doe."

The mule-deer shakes its head back and forth, flopping its ears all around.

"I know. I say that every year. Hey, I haven't met anyone either. So, don't you feel so bad about yourself." Without anyone to talk to, Kip had grown quite fond of the animal throughout each year's escapades. Even when he isn't talking the beast's floppy ears off, they enjoy meandering through the lush landscapes and brilliantly lit-up skies together in silence.

Some people like to marvel and gawk at expansive landscape paintings and critique each brush stroke. Not Kip—he prefers to experience the beauty firsthand. There is no substitute for the freshness of a morning's dew glistening against a new sunrise.

"Well, here's hoping we don't end up stag again...no offense."

The mule-deer scratches at the floor with a defiant hoof in response.

"Yeah. I also say that joke every year, don't I?" With a slight tug on the reins, they are off again to yet another stale adventure.

Kip has no idea what is in store for him this year, and he cannot wait any longer for his own greatness to prevail.

Day Two, 7:35 am: Exhaustion

The morning light came in hard and much too fast for Kip's liking. After tossing and turning for the better part of the night, he wasn't at all ready for another day of the festival.

He never should have had any alcohol last night. Something about the fermentation process makes him feel like he has been hit in the face by a maul whenever he drinks. The heaviness behind his eyes distorts the world and makes it seem as though everything is in the background. It's hard to focus on anything.

For some reason, he thought last night was going to be different—a fun-filled evening of mingling with the event-goers, establishing contacts, and possibly creating lasting friendships.

The throbbing pain in his head says

otherwise. Everything is a blur when he tries to remember how he got back to his room in the inn or what happened after he downed the fermented poison. It is all vague and distant. All he wanted was to feel better, but now he feels way worse.

Before getting himself something to calm the acidity that is burning the inside of his stomach, Kip makes his way past the great arena and back to the stables to tend to his companion. Priorities are important, and putting himself behind others is one of his.

While unlatching the stable gate, he can hear the far-off excitement from his mule-deer, eager for breakfast.

"Settle down. I'm coming." Kip covers his nose, smelling the awful stench of the other less attentive pet owner's stables. To some, these beasts are property, a means of travel, food, and income—much less than an equal. To Kip, however, his pet is family, the only family he has for a hundred miles and the only one that didn't run him out of town.

Kip wonders how the beast always knows when he is around. Smelling his shoulder, he knows it couldn't be his scent—he still reeks of booze from the previous night. It could possibly be the sound of his step, or perhaps he behaves this way when anyone comes by, and Kip just so happens to see it when he's around. Kip rather likes to think that the deer has magical sight that allows him to see right through solid objects. No matter the reason, it makes him feel special, especially believing that his mule-deer is capable of any such extraordinary ability, no matter now unlikely it may seem to some.

Keeping his head low, Kip rushes past the hungry eyes and licking chops from the gauntlet of neglected working animals. His caring nature has taught him to pretend they don't exist or else he might share all of his tidbits and treats, leaving nothing for his old friend.

A sweet whining from a passing cage almost catches his gaze, though he shields his face and the urge with his hand. His stride turns to a double-step until he reaches the soft muzzle of his long-horned friend. "Sorry I'm late. I had quite a night," Kip says, rolling his eyes to the sky.

The deer's head flops to the side inquisitively.

"No, nothing like that..."

The deer responds by gently tugging at the bag hanging off Kip's shoulder.

"Okay, okay. Give me a moment." Kip rummages through the tote, reaching for his pet's very favorite—speckled corn.

The mule-deer stamps his hooves excitedly while waiting for his pampered breakfast.

Creeping out from the next stall, a giraffe neck stretches out of a chamber as far as it will go—desperately trying to steal a morsel. His long tongue extends out over Kip's shoulder and snatches a branch right out of his bag.

"Hey! Give that back."

Like a turtle, the giraffe retracts its neck back from whence it came, out of sight, with victory on its lips.

"I suppose that's okay. I did bring a little extra," Kip says with a glare.

Not wanting to get pickpocketed by another starving animal, Kip removes the rope latch to the chamber gate and quickly makes his way inside—protectively gripping his sack of goodies.

Still chomping on the corn, the deer shivers upon feeling Kips gentle fingers stroking its fur.

"See, there's no way that freedom could treat you so well." Kip knows that none of this stuff grows remotely close to each other, and his mule-deer could never have such a varied spread in the wild.

"Apple for your thoughts?" Kip says, handing the deer a fist-apple—a fruit that not only looks like a balled-up hand but also has a splendid bitterness that packs a punch.

Kip puts his arm around the animal and breathes in his musky scent. "But I *will* set you free someday. I promise."

Day Four, 6:06 am: A Bad Promise

Flames heat up the air as balls of fire hurl through the morning sky. Sunspots form in Kip's vision from briefly looking at the scorching sky.

This is much different than what he experienced earlier. So much has changed since he has been away, or so he thinks.

He never should have left. Saving one person doesn't justify leaving the rest. But he was lost in a glance and doomed from the start.

A larger than normal fireball tears through the sky, missing any notable targets. It is way off course. It looks like it's heading...

"Please, no!" Kip has no time to think about a strategy to stop such an attack; it's just cruel. He runs without thinking, pushing and shoving signs and stacks of hay barrels out of his way.

His purpose in returning topside was to make sure his friends were all safe, and now someone close to him is in danger.

Kip's fears are actualized as he witnesses the roof of the stables ablaze. Never has he ever wanted to be more wrong in his life than in this instant. The mysterious flames that were burning up the sky just made things personal.

"No!" Kip slams into the old door shoulder first.

Smoke escapes through the slats and uneven workmanship. The fire is too late to stop. The hay and alfalfa are dry and ignite instantaneously.

Kip hears the stamping feet of all the scared livestock inside—the neighing of horses and other working animals, the low guttural cry of a camel and, of course, he can hear the throatier bleat of his mule-deer—he is scared, so scared.

"Don't worry, I'm coming." Kip tries to open the latch, but it burns his hand instantly. The metal is already heated up. The fire must be right behind the door.

Blowing on his hand doesn't begin to ease the tender sting of blisters forming.

There is a sudden urge to break down, to hide away in the consuming pain of it all.

Instead, he bangs against the door, over and over again, though it doesn't open. The structure is still too strong and intact, for now. This is taking too much time. If he is going to save his friend, he has to be quicker, stronger...something other than himself.

"Help! Help!" he cries, looking for assistance, but no one is around to notice him.

Again, he tries the metal latch, trying to force himself through the agonizing pain. Never has he felt such a debilitating sensation. He's literally cooking his flesh while he's still alive. Kip screams through the searing pain, with tears burning his eyes. He gives it all he can, until he cannot—not anymore.

The fire is so hot that it must have fused the latch to the clasp.

Feeling outside of this world, Kip looks down at his blistered skin on his hand. It looks deformed, and he didn't even get the lock open.

Giving up on this fool's errand, Kip rushes a carriage up the hill from the stable. It is a long jaunt, but Kip has no time to rest his legs.

Ignoring his singed hand, he pushes it from behind. The adrenaline coursing through him makes him feel as though he has giant-like strength as he dislodges it from its parked position.

Before it gets away from him, Kip climbs aboard the carriage to see this thing through to the bitter end. Holding on to the straps, he is ready for bravery. He only has one shot at this, and he could never push it back into position again if it fails. The stables look so small from here, but not for long.

The metal-lined wagon wheels start to pick up momentum as they fly down the steep hill. It is a bumpy ride, with the wheels rattling and shaking against the cobblestone street.

The carriage starts to veer off course.

"No, no, no, no, no." He turns the straps towards the stables, but it isn't turning. He notices horse brushes, saddles, and other accessories. Without a horse pulling the carriage, there is no way to control the thing.

"Stupid. What was I thinking?" This whole plan isn't working the way he thought it should.

Still careening down the hill, he climbs to where the straps are connected and unhooks them from their wooden frame. His intention is to redirect the wheels somehow, which have some movement from left to right.

It is a long road, but the end of the line is approaching fast. He better make quick work of this if he wants to survive his trip.

He twirls the strap around like a lasso and throws it at the front wheel's hubcap. The friction from the spinning wheel slaps away his insolence.

The cart is driving even further off course, right towards a giant pyramid of hay. It might soften his collision, but it will also not do.

Again, he throws the strap at the wheel. This time, it gets caught and entangled inside the wooden spokes. It's not exactly what he had planned.

Kip is pulled right into the wheel well. The world spins as it chomps him up like he is inside a dragon's mouth. Before his body can register all the pain, it spits him out.

His eyes are half open as the carriage runs right into the stables, knocking down the door. Flames erupt out of the opening, and the carriage is now starting to burn along with it.

His body is too banged up at the moment to even move.

Is every bone in my body broken?

Then out of the stables bound horses, goats, and donkeys, all flee from the scene. He did it!

"A promise is a promise." Kip says through blood-lined teeth.

One after another, singed animals flee for their lives. The fire must have burned the ropes that held them inside their stables.

"Where is he?" Kip eagerly awaits the one he came here to save, but the mule-deer isn't within his sight. The herd is already starting to thin out. A pile of burning wood collapses from the roof, partially blocking the exit.

His friend isn't coming out. Maybe he's trapped.

Placing a shaky hand on the base of an oil-lamp post, Kip pulls himself up, the pain of his injuries leaving him completely crippled.

Slowly he makes his way towards the stables. His stride has changed to a limp, with him dragging one of his legs behind.

With one hand shielding his eyes and the other covering his face, he presses on, right into the burning structure, ducking under the rafters that have fallen against the cart.

The air is dense, and the only thing he can see is the bright contrasting flames against the black smoke. Each flame moves with a devastating excitement that is overwhelming. Almost like a living, breathing entity.

Faintly, he hears a distant cry. It is muffled by the cracking and popping of the raging inferno.

"Hello? Is someone down there?"

"Over here!" the voice squeaks.

A person? That isn't what Kip was expecting to find. He has to do something. They must be trapped.

Forging ahead, Kip tries to locate the faint sound. Time is running out. The flames are growing to the ceiling, and the wood around him shifts and creaks as if it were a boat on the Sea of Tears.

As if an unknown force is guiding him there, he finds a figure in the back of the stable that has yet to be engulfed with flames. Wrapped up in blankets, it appears to be a young stable hand—a boy. He is breathing through a small hole in the lower right corner of the stable. Kip gets down low and joins him for a quick breath.

"Are you hurt?" Kip asks between breaths.

"My papa, he was supposed to come back for me."

"There is no one in here—no one alive."

"I am in here," the boy protests.

Kip realizes that that was, indeed, a poor choice of words. Technically the boy is right. They are both alive and in here. It isn't beyond the realm of possibility that there could be more survivors, but he seriously doubts it.

"What I meant to say is that I didn't see anyone else. As it was, I barely found you." Kip can't help but let out some heavy coughs.

"I always wanted to be cremated when I died, but not while I'm still alive," the long-haired boy admits with dried tear streaks on his dirt-ridded face.

"You shouldn't be thinking of such things. You're not going to die. Not while I'm here." Kip hadn't thought about his own death until a couple years ago. One of the best parts about being young is not worrying about the future—being hopeful and carefree. But when you reach a certain age, it becomes all you obsess over.

The boy gives Kip a look of uncertainty. "But...I already said my goodbyes."

"Well, it is time to say hello again."

With a quivering hand over his mouth, the boy says, "No. I've given up."

The fire makes its way to the chamber door, blocking their escape. Time is already working against them, and it is almost up.

"Well, like it or not, I never give up." Kip picks up a wash bucket that still has a little water inside it and splashes the boy with it.

"That's hot. Why would you do something

like..."

Without answering, Kip tosses him onto his shoulder and leaps through the wall of flames that's blocking their path. Suddenly, Kip no longer notices his lame leg or anything other than his task at hand. He is determined and focused.

Kip dodges and weaves through the burning hallway as the boy kicks and screams. The smoke is so thick that all he can do is avoid the burning bits and trust in his memory to escape.

It feels as if the fire is at his heels, chasing him with a mind of its own—a predator hungry for consumption.

The fire is now everywhere—on the floor, crawling up the walls, encasing the felled logs lining the floor. He dances around the flames, which feel like hands reaching out to grab them both. Soon he bounds out of the stables, nearly tripping over his own feet.

Dropping the stable boy on the ground, he notices the blankets he is wrapped in are smoking.

Frantically, he pats the boy down to make sure there are no active embers. Even though Kip dowsed him with water, his clothes are now completely dry, and his hair looks crunchy.

A small flame ignites on the horse blanket wrapped around the boy.

In one fluid motion, Kip rips the blanket off the boy and bangs it against the ground—swatting endlessly until it stops smoking.

"Thank you," the boy says, breaking Kip's assault on the small fire that is clearly out.

Kip looks at the boy with renewed eyes. This isn't a boy at all. The boy he saved is actually a little girl—wearing a horse-print skirt and fine buckled shoes.

"I'm sorry. I thought..." Visibility was low inside the barn, and the fire was intense. There is no fault in Kip making that mistake.

She flashes him a little smile. The funny thing about smiling is that it is very contagious, and Kip is infected by her happiness.

Although this moment is pure and heart-warming, it only lasts a quick moment before Kip remembers his mule-deer. Saving this child has cost him greatly.

Scrambling to rush back inside the blazing structure, the girl grabs ahold of his good leg.

"You can't go back in there."

"I must!"

"No. You'll get all burned up."

Kip pulls and kicks, but she isn't letting go.

"I...don't...care...now let me go!"

"You saved me. Now I'm saving you."

She's right. He is too late. The fire is engulfing the whole structure, leaving nothing untouched by the flames' greedy fingers. Defeat loosens his shoulders and he slumps over, straining to keep his eyes fixed on the blaze. There is no more time for heroic flame-dancing.

"Come on, boy. You can do this," Kip whispers, knowing that it is up to his mule-deer to save himself now. Kip sticks four fingers into his mouth and whistles as loud as he can—exhausting the last of his breath in one hard motion. The sound is sharp and at an ear-piercing volume.

The little girl is covering her ears with her hands.

While on their journey together, Kip has a no-leash policy for his companion. He lets the deer run wild during breaks and while they make camp. This is the very same call he uses to draw the deer back again.

In towns and cities, however, residents don't allow for such things as free-running animals and crack-of-dawn deer calling. As a result, Kip must rent a stable or other confinement to ease their minds.

Once he rented a room with a vaulted ceiling and intentionally snuck his pet in at night. They couldn't exactly snuggle up like they would on the cold nights in the wild. Oil lamps got knocked over, and there was an antler-sized rip in the bedding.

Sneaking him out was a harder task, and the local authorities ended up running them both out of town before he could collect all of his belongings.

Remembering the good times only makes things worse for Kip emotionally.

Just when he almost completely loses hope, an animal leaps through the firestorm. Its antlers are the only part not completely consumed by flames as it runs for its life. Smoke trails off the large flames like silk from a spider.

The fire got him, and he is fighting for survival.

Holding the horse blanket, Kip rushes to aid his mount. There is a fountain filled with water not too far away from the stables. He hopes his friend can make it there in time to put himself out and put Kip's own regret to rest.

First, Kip tries to block the animal's path and run him down. This doesn't work.

The beast is running in the wrong direction. How would it know about fire and water or how to put itself out?

Kip has a sudden pang of guilt wash over him.

The fire seems to be forcing the thing to flee blindly in any direction. It keeps doubling back just out of Kip's reach. In the end, it is just an animal, despite all the intelligence Kip has put on him.

Waving his hand and twirling the blanket, Kip tries to urge his friend in the right direction. There is no way Kip can get the animal to understand what he is trying to do. It is much too scared and hurt.

Accidentally, Kip is caught in a rib by an antler. He falls to the ground, grabbing at his side, as if he has been hit by the hard truth. He cannot move. The pain is too intense. His body far passed exhausted.

Picking up where Kip left off, the stable girl snatches the blanket out of his hand and tries to drive the animal to the fountain. She calls and cries out to the thing, but it just won't listen.

The deer runs and runs until the fire is too much, and it falls to one knee.

Kip wants nothing else but to help, but he is too hurt to move.

Swatting at the animal with the smoking blanket, the girl tries to extinguish the flames.

"Get up, please, old friend," Kip says through his broken voice.

The deer's movement becomes slow like molasses, as he tries to get up but ultimately can't.

The girl doesn't give up. Over and over she swats. But this isn't any normal fire. It is magically infused somehow, making it only burn more with each wave of the blanket.

Soon the flames are roaring so high that she is forced to step out of arm's reach. She buckles, hiding her cries in the fetal position.

"I am sorry. So very sorry. You were always my favorite person...stag."

Slowly the deer bows its head, and Kip watches as he turns to ash and bone. As horrifying as it is for Kip to witness, he makes sure that his friend doesn't enter the afterlife alone.

Kip's actions saved all the animals of the stables, except the one that matters to him the most. No victory can fill the hole inside his heart that this failure has created. Mistakes are choices that one must live with, and this is one that Kip would take to his grave, sooner rather than later.

When the World Falls Down

"I didn't want to speak about all the things I bore witness to.

"Does ignoring their pain make me a selfish person? Normally, I deal with my own darkness through laughter—a way to turn my feelings inside out. I just hide behind a smile and cry through each chuckle. But not today. This was no laughing matter. I owed them that much.

"Huddled together, we became a family while hunkering through the storm of storms. In the end, only I remain.

"The shower of tears that I spilled on the red cobblestones made a pink trail. My pain is far less than those who leaked before me. In both cases, we left all of ourselves behind.

"This is a time to think positive, to regroup and remember the victims for what they are going to be henceforth—immortalized.

"If I can remember their names and their smiling faces, so can the rest of the world. Only then will they live on forever, like a grand fable, or timeless joke. I will not let them be forgotten. I shoulder the responsibility, because they are my family. This is serious business.

"Garo, Wild Bell, Chani, Tess, Peldu, Ko-Ki, I shout each person's name, and describe the features of the ones I don't know for sure. With their memory on my mind, I charge in head-first, gripping my weapon with both hands—bells ringing. This is how I pay homage to their sacrifice. This is what the mortals will remember me by." -*Perkins, The Court Jester, age 24.*

Day Three, 4:54 pm: A Small Voice

Mounds of bodies are scattered around the battlefield.

Kip rushes to the nearest body and places his hand on its neck. "Damn." This one is cold to the touch. This is his method of figuring out who's alive and who's slain.

Reaching into his bag, he marks it by placing

a shredded white cloth over its head. This reduces the chance of anyone doing double work and also makes his job easier without all those scary faces looking back at him.

He continues on to the next one only to find the same outcome. One after another, he sifts through the corpses looking for survivors—still nothing. Without the help of the healers, this area has suffered far more casualties.

Around the time he is just about to give up hope, he hears a faint cry.

"Is someone around?"

"Over here. Please help me."

Kip brings his ear low to the ground.

"If you can hear me, keep talking."

One by one, Kip flips over bodies, looking to find where the little voice is coming from. Laying white cloth everywhere, he has to be getting closer, but he still cannot find the source of the cries. Changing direction, he figures that he has been heading the wrong way.

"I am stuck. I cannot move," says the faint voice once more.

"Keep going. I am coming for you." Kip moves quietly like a cat, trying his darndest not to stumble over her words.

"What do you want me to say?"

"Anything. Just give me some clues as to where to find you."

"I can't see anything. It is so dark. I am worried."

Puzzled, Kip looks up at the defused sunlight that is shining on the streets. "That's okay. Just tell me something."

"Like what?"

"What brought you to the festival?"

"I got married yesterday."

"Congratulations. What did you wear?" Kip turns over a corpse that is missing a face. He places his hand over his mouth, stopping himself from throwing up at the horrendous sight. Then, he lets a cloth feather down onto what wasn't there.

"A tapered dress, white and innocent. It was my mother's. We had to make quite a few adjustments in order for it to fit my frame. You see, she was pregnant with my brother when she first got married. That's why we needed the alteration."

"That sounds really nice." Kip scrambles around, trying to pinpoint her location.

He is getting closer. "Tell me more about it."

A hissing sound echoes throughout the castle. This is something new. Something horrible.

Her muffled voice screams.

Kip ducks down and closes his eyes tight. *It is starting again.* He is as motionless as the rest of the deceased.

Casually crawling down the street is a thick fog. It blocks out the light as it moves, and it is moving straight towards Kip.

"Hello? Are you still out there? What is that noise? I'm so scared," she says hysterically.

Kip is also scared of the dark and ominous creeping doom. He knows that she is relying on him to save her. This is no time for him to break down.

Taking his frustration out on the ground, Kip slams his fist. Instantly, he feels discomfort in his hand where it connected with the hard cobblestone. Gripping his hand, he tries to stop the pain from starting, but it is too late.

No. I can't let this stop me. Time is running out. If he is ever going to find her, it has to be right now or it will certainly be never. "Yes, I didn't leave you. Listen to my voice. It will be okay." Kip tries to make his voice sound reassuring, even though he is doubting his odds. "Just tell me about your husband."

"Okay. It's quite funny. I never thought I'd find love, especially when my parents have been arranging the ceremony since I was a little girl." Her voice calms.

"But you did, didn't you? Find love, that is?"

"I am ashamed to say that, at first, I wasn't sure. I am a wimp when it comes to this stuff. I was scared about marriage. Isn't that silly, I mean, I've known him my whole life."

"If you felt that way, it's not silly; it's honest."

"I recited the words, but I didn't mean them the way he did…" She lets out a sigh.

He is getting close. "Go on."

"Except I truly mean them now. My feelings came late, but they did come…completely."

Kip turns over an oaf of a man and sees two baby blue eyes on a woman staring back at him. For a moment, she blinks at him in disbelief. She's lying on her stomach in an innocent tapered dress that is no longer white. She has a crown of wildflowers interlaced with her large ringlet curls.

"I found you." Kip's voice cracks, and he coughs, trying to hide his happiness for finding her in time.

Her young smile is worth more than any reward or monetary compensation someone could give him. He feels like a prince saving a princess.

Both their hands connect, and Kip pulls her up to her feet. They take a couple steps when...

"Wait..."

"What is it?" Kip asks, as she slips through his fingers.

"When the chaos started, he threw himself on top of me. He gave his life for mine." The young bride collapses to the side of the man who was just protecting her.

She kisses her two fingers and gently presses them to his cold lips. "You kept your promise. 'Until death, you shall give love,'" she says softly, removing a single flower from her hair.

"We have to go." Kip ducks down as some dark mist floats past his head, a little too close for his comfort.

"...and I will keep mine to you."

"Let's leave right now," Kip says, feeling bad about interrupting her heartfelt goodbye.

The bride drapes herself over the man who gave himself to her.

Her look says everything. It shows how she feels ashamed for doubting her husband during their vows. Only in death has he proved to be the exact love she had been dreaming about.

Kip wants to try and pull the newlyweds apart, but he is overwhelmed by this moment. Real love has grown out of the tragedy of the night, even though it was too short-lived.

Day One, 7:45 pm: Poison in a Glass

Kip's feet are as heavy as bricks and sore to the touch. Most of the damage was done from his long journey trying to reach the festival, but after a whole day of being on his feet, the pain has only gotten worse. Things started to pick up in the late afternoon, and he's feeling the results.

All he wants is to soak his feet in a warm bucket of water. After shaking so many customers' hands, Kip is starting to feel as though he's coming down with something. Festival Flu is a common illness that people get from attending these types of events. When you have thousands of people from different regions and walks of life together in such confined spaces, it's only natural for illnesses to become rampant.

The mood has changed drastically from the sunlight hours. Drinks are flowing, and belligerence from overindulgence is becoming a more common occurrence. People are loud and proud of it.

Not wanting anything to do with the party crowd, Kip looks to find some sort of herbal shop before hitting the hay. In truth, he sprang for a higher-quality inn this time around, and he'll be, more accurately, hitting the "silk" tonight.

In the corner, he notices a man holding a woman's hair back as she vomits up the liquor that she can no longer handle. No doubt it's one of the festival's specialty drinks that is served inside a hollowed-out melon of some kind. A trail of bluish-green liquid snakes between the cobblestones towards a floor drain. Kip flashes the gentleman an encouraging smile as he admires the kindness.

The man returns with a gesture that says, "What can you do?" The woman starts to cough heavily, and the man turns his attention back to her, leans in closer, and whispers some sweet nothings into her ear.

With only a burp as a warning, the man projectile vomits next to the woman, getting bits and pieces in her hair and all over her fashionable dress.

Kip's cringe is unmistakably present on his

face. He did not except that to happen.

While still dry heaving, herself, the woman contorts her arm to pat the man on the back in a comforting way. She's returning the sympathetic favor despite what just happened.

Kip's frown quickly turns back into an adoring smile. As disgusting as it is, this is what he has always wanted. No, not to drink himself sick, but to find someone to share his unconditional caring with—someone to stick by him at his worst possible moments. Everyone has low lows, but to share them with someone somehow makes it all better.

A few intersections and winding corridors later, Kip arrives at his destination. A faded, splintery sign vaguely reads, "The Sea Witch's Apothecary."

Upon entering the musky building, an out-of-tune bell alerts a sleeping man behind the counter of his customer's presence.

The shopkeeper jostles himself awake amid a loud snort. "Hello, I'm Keve, and welcome to my a..." he says, leading into a deep yawn. "...pothecary."

"Are you the sea witch?" Kip cannot help but ask as an attempt at humor.

Keve grabs at his long silver hair—that, in

Kip's defense, does resemble the stereotypical witch look—before letting it fall back to his shoulders mid-stretch.

"No. she lives in the sea." Keve smacks his dry lips. "What's your poison, friend?"

"No, no. Not here for that. I just…" Kip starts. His voice is hoarse and cracks as he struggles to get even the simplest of words out.

"Convention crud?"

With his mouth agape, Kip sizes himself up and down, looking for the contagious rash. "I don't think so. Geez, I hope not."

"Oh, must be fest flu, then," Keve says matter-of-factly, already rummaging through some jars behind the counter.

"Unfortunately, yeah."

"It never misses festival."

"Also, do you have any salm…"

Blindly, Keve throws a vial over his right shoulder towards Kip.

Not ready for the throw, Kip flounders to catch it. It's like watching a cat trying to swim—terrified and scrambling to get back to dry ground.

Bouncing off his forearm, the bottle topples to the floor, and luckily it doesn't break. There is a small crack, however, and the liquid is already starting to seep out.

"This will do the trick," Keve says, bracing himself against a chair as he tries to stand up again. He lets out the traditional sound older people make when they're forced to move too much. It's one part sigh to two parts groan, with a dash of cracking old bones mixed in.

As a ploy to hide his failure to catch the treatment, Kip quickly pops the cork, and in one solid gulp, he finishes off the contents. It tastes strongly of mint and burns all the way down to his toes.

"Well, well. What are you doing?"

Wiping his chin with his sleeve, Kip readies himself to tell a smooth joke or a snappy one-liner. He knows the shopkeeper must be impressed. Kip ends up coughing uncontrollably instead of wowing Keve with a suave statement.

"You were not supposed to drink it. It's a topical anesthetic to apply to your hands after you meet people."

Kip's eyes grow wide as he examines his shaky hands. "What?" A little bit of drool leaks out of his slack-jawed mouth. "Am I going to die? I feel funny." He doesn't know if it's all in his head or not, but a warm feeling washes over him as if it's traveling straight through his veins.

"I honestly don't know. No one has ever done *that* before."

Spitting in his hand, Kip starts to spread his saliva all over his exposed skin for some strange reason. When that isn't working fast enough, he has another plan.

"Are you hungry?" Keve asks, looking quite concerned.

"You 'thed it twas topical," Kip says while licking his forearm.

"Not like that, man," Keve says, shaking his head back and forth. "I have more of it, you know."

Frantically, Kip starts to scratch at his forearm as it goes numb.

"I can't feel anything. What's in it?" Kip asks, swaying back and forth.

"A little of this, a little of that, and a lot of alcohol."

"You mean like what's in those...cute little fancy drinks?" Kip asks, slurring his speech and holding up a finger, as if perfectly on cue.

"No. Much, much worse."

Kip holds back a gasp, as a pang of nausea is unsettling his stomach. He is going to keep it together, and everything is going to be fine.

Instead, he says the first thing that comes to mind. "Do you like me? Why don't people like me?"

Day Three, 5:05 pm: A Little Less Than More

The battling adventurers have not been seen or heard from for nearly twelve hours. Even without their protection, Kip knows he is safe for the time being. He uses this respite to try and do some good in the aftermath, just like the false knight had instructed. There is no way of knowing if the rest of the resistance fighters have joined the knight in his sacrificial glory, although in their absence, things are looking bleak.

A thick haze continuously drifts through the streets with purpose, like a snake slithering through a garden, hungry for death. The once brilliant light that burned the sky is streaking colors against the thick, obscuring fog. Everything looks as though it's covered in oil.

He looks back to see the newlywed couple still in their embrace. The bride raises up her hand in defiance, standing up to the tyranny of the day. The dark fog swallows them whole.

The creeping darkness is much too thick to determine if it has harmed the bride or not. Kip is too scared to find out for himself.

Like a rat desperate to survive the serpent, Kip takes to the low ground. He's making his way through the maze of people and corpses alike. A few coughs and hacks respond to the arrival of the approaching vapor. It is strenuous to see through, hard to breathe, and sour to smell.

"What is this?" a faint voice echoes in the distance.

"The end of life," another responds.

Reduced to a crawl, Kip climbs over a corpse.

"Rest in peace," he whispers, hoping that any spirits that might be around know that he means no disrespect. Death and the dead are never something he is ever going to be comfortable being around.

While climbing over a second body, it grabs his arm tightly.

"I'm sorry...very sorry. I thought..."

"I was dead? Get your paws off me and my coins," the corpse responds, letting Kip know how wrong his assumption was.

"That was not my intention...I..." Kip is truly

offended that someone would think that, in a time like this, anyone would stoop so low as to pickpocket. Then again, he has seen it with his own eyes.

"Then explain why you're climbing all over me. I doubt it's to ask me for a date."

"To be honest, you were not moving and..."

"And you wanted to gain a fortune off my misfortune? Admit it."

"No! I was crawling over you because I wanted to keep my clothes dry," Kip says, nodding over at a lump with a gaping crater in its torso that is filled with red liquid.

With a struggle and a grunt, the corpse man pries open one eye to observe Kip's alibi. His red eye squints and strains as his grip on Kip tightens even further.

"I'm telling the truth," Kip asserts.

"Where were you heading in such a hurry?"

"To help someone. I just had to get away from this fog. That is why I am so low."

"Why?"

"I've seen...terrible things. Who knows if this stuff is some kind of a plague...or worse," Kip stammers.

"I see."

"Will you let me go now?" Kip flinches, as

the fog lingers above them.

"There are two types of people in this world: those who want to save the world, and those who want to save themselves. One cannot exist without destroying the other. So, which kind of person are you?"

Caught in a trap, Kip starts searching his mind for the correct answer to free himself from this man's grasp. "Well, um...I..."

"Level with me; you weren't trying to save anyone other than yourself."

"Ok. I admit that I wanted to save myself first. Then I *was* planning on helping others. That is the honest truth."

"Not good enough."

Just then, a woman's voice cries out, "Hey, leave me alone. Let go of me. I'm married."

What follows is the sound of a scuffle. It is coming from the direction of the newlywed couple.

"You're going to be married to me now," a lower voice responds.

Tension is high, and victims seem to be turning on each other instead of joining forces to help each other. At this rate, no one is going to survive if people don't stop destroying each other's safety and, instead, take a stand against the predators who prey on the weak.

It doesn't take a stretch of the imagination for Kip to get what is going to happen here.

"Let me go, please. I can help her," Kip pleads with the alive corpse who has him in something stronger than a death grip.

"Right after you save yourself? Don't pretend to play the hero now, kid. I caught you in a lie."

Jerking and tugging, Kip tries to free himself from the corpse-man's grasp, but his hold is ironclad.

Sharp, loud, thunderous sounds fill the area and silence the woman's cries. Something new is starting, something that sounds just as awful as before, if not worse. It is a continuous sound that rings loudly like bells. The noise is rhythmic, each one marching after the next in perfect succession.

"Let me do something. Please," Kip asks one last time. To his surprise, the man who holds him as a hostage releases him—not because he sees the tears welling up in Kip's eyes, because now he really is dead. A thin line of blood streaks out of the corpse's mouth.

As part of his routine, Kip places a white cloth over the man's face.

"Don't worry, we're just going to have a little fun," says the same voice as before.

A thought crosses Kip's mind—a dreadful, unforgiving thought that he regrets having instantly. But he knows he has to act on his idea, no matter the consequence or how it makes him feel.

Slow and steady, he moves his fingers in and around the corpse-man's clothes, who is actually now just a man corpse.

Kip knows that the if the man was protesting so much the idea of Kip being a thief, that only means he must have something on him worth stealing.

Technically, it isn't stealing if the man isn't alive—it's looting. Still, that doesn't make it any better or make Kip feel any less horrible about doing it. Most of all, he feels the worst about becoming the exact person the man erroneously pegged him to be.

Digging deep into his pockets, there are a fair number of gems and other valuables that will not serve Kip any in this doomsday scenario. No, he needs something sharp and, hopefully, magical.

Patting the man down, Kip finds a wet spot that has to be from the hole that killed him.

Liquid is leaking out of him, still warm with the life that was there moments before.

Normally Kip is terrified of any or all blood-borne illnesses, and out of habit, he quickly retreats his hand. Going back in, he moves his busy fingers down the man's leg and on to his boot. Inside he finds a slim dagger. Unlike normal daggers, this one has no hilt or handle. Instead, it has a blade at both ends, which means that it is made for throwing. This is the exact thing he is looking for and wanted to find. The only thing is, he doesn't ever want to use it for its intended purpose—to kill someone.

With the sporadic ringing sounds at his back, Kip scrambles back to where the newly-wed couple was. Just like he guessed, she is gone. Relying again on his ears, he follows the faint sounds of the woman's whimpers. Her quiet sobs act as breadcrumbs in the dark, foggy sky.

Unlike last time, he moves silently so as not to give away his position.

He can't quite pinpoint her exact location without standing up and getting a better perspective, but he isn't about to do something as foolish or brazen as that. Or is he?

Taking in a lasting deep breath, he then runs

through the fog headfirst. It feels wet and cold, and so thick that he might as well be running blind. But closing his eyes would do him no good. He has to be alert to avoid the red splotches that are staining the fog like a painter's palette. He doesn't know where they are coming from or why, but he doesn't dare touch whatever it is.

He needs to breathe eventually, but he continues forward nonetheless. There might not be any lasting effects this stuff has on your insides, but that is a chance he isn't willing to take.

Starved for air, he drops to the ground—taking in a couple fresh gulps while he can. His hands grip something soft on the ground. It is some kind of animal skin or rug.

"Stop it. You're hurting me!" the bride says. Her voice is clear as day. They are close, too close.

Without thinking, Kip tosses the throwing blade in the direction of her voice. The fog parts out of its way as the blade soars.

It connects with something, and after a loud thud, everything goes quiet.

What did I do? That was a stupid shot in the dark. Kip recounts the moment he nearly threw his dagger at a guard when he was contemplating stopping the voucher thief.

There is no time for him to regret his decision, not yet. Following the lead of the flying dagger, he bounds to his feet and uses the fur-lined fabric as a fan, waving the fog up to the sky.

It appears to be working, as a clear tunnel is soon in view. The stuff is lighter than air and looks softer than silk as it is being blown away.

Parting the way forward, he follows the path of his dagger until he finally sees her...

Standing alone, she is using a handkerchief to do the same thing as him, making a tunnel for herself.

They both seem pleasantly surprised to see each other, sharing the same hopeful expression as if they were looking at each other through a mirror.

He gives her a shrug as if to say "great minds think alike."

Suddenly, it's as though all the death around them is gone as they share a laugh.

The front of her not-so-white dress is moist with tears.

In this light, she is so innocent, with skin as smooth as a pearl. Kip is captivated by her. They share a moment outside of everything. It is safe, and secure, and...over.

A round of explosive volleys flies through the courtyard. It must be getting closer now.

Instantly, she hides her face inside her hands. Her body shakes and cringes with each jolt. The pleasantness of the moment is gone as reality sinks in.

"I am here. You're safe," Kip says to the young bride, hoping to ease her desperation some. He doesn't even know if she can hear him through the sounds assaulting the air.

Their look is over, and she seems far-past the point of being consolable.

Finally, when the volley ceases, she turns her head to the sky as if looking for something— most likely an angel to escort her to the after-life. Her glassy-eyed expression says it all. She is doing all that she has left in her, waiting for death, in order to rejoin her husband.

"Where is he—the man who tried to hurt you?" Kip asks but is met with no answer. "I really must know."

"No."

Out of nowhere, another round of blasts fills the courtyard. Kip leaps on the woman and wraps her into his arms tightly, dropping them both to the ground.

She isn't in the right headspace to be sitting out there in the open like that. It is lucky that she wasn't hit last time, and he doesn't want to chance it for another round.

He feels her nails digging into his side, breaking through his skin. She is scared, and her trembling hand makes her nails dig in even deeper.

Kip doesn't blame her one bit; he is also scared, but for an entirely different reason. For the first time ever, the stabbing pain is comforting. It is as if he's taking her pain and burden onto himself, and in this one incident, he can handle this type of hurt. For her, he can endure it all.

Things are shattering all around their embrace—projectiles screaming above them in all directions, cutting holes into the remaining fog and letting the outside sunshine sneak in.

After this round hammers out its destruction, Kip places her face between his hands and asks again. "Please tell me. If he is out there, I need to stop him. What if he tries something like that again?"

This time her eyes flutter open with some life to them.

"Did he...hurt you?"

She shakes her head back and forth, wiping a couple stray tears from her eyes. A streak of blood from her finger smudges her cheek.

Licking his thumb, Kip wipes away the smudge mark in an endearing way.

She sniffles and bites her lip.

"Can you walk?" Kip asks her.

She looks back at him with the purity of a child but the years of a woman. She has such sweetness about her, masked by an unforgettable sadness.

"Today's my wedding day."

"I know. I am sorry this happened."

"Can you please get me out of here?"

"Well...um..." Kip quickly curbs himself. He doesn't want to give her a disappointing response. All he wants is to make her smile, make her give him that look she gave that moment they saw each other.

Tears slowly make their way across her cheeks again.

She may not be physically injured, but emotionally she's paralyzed. And now, in turn, so is he.

She is soft and sweet, and as much as Kip would love to gaze into her light blue eyes for eternity, he isn't going to give up so easily. "Of course I will," he swears.

Once more, the onslaught of projectiles comes, beating their melodic, explosive drums. And just like before, they wrap into each other in an embrace. This time, giving in to his emotions, Kip squeezes on to her almost as tightly as she to him. Their chests beat against each other, and suddenly they don't feel so alone. It is as if they've known each other since the beginning of time. Or perhaps this is the moment time began again.

Cringing through the racket, Kip waits for the familiar ringing in his ears to regain himself. The woman's smooth, wet cheek is against his. He wants to stay there, to believe that he found someone to share his life with, if only for a couple moments.

This isn't about him. It is much bigger than that. For whatever he feels for her in this moment, it is real, pure, and is forcing him to become better than who he currently is—a coward looking to save himself, not the world. This transformation is not for himself, but for her and the look she is giving him right now.

It takes all he has to break away from those eyes. Deep down he knows he isn't worthy of those long batting eyelashes, and her heart belongs to her dead husband. But he *will* save her innocence...or die trying.

Danger Sculpts the Soul

"No matter tenan or venan, the path is visibly clear. I don't fight for victory; I only aim to entertain.

"The past cannot be undone, but the future is a vicious thread that needs to be unraveled and burned at both ends. It's much too late for what-ifs. Regret is a preventative emotion to ensure that you don't make the same mistake twice, but what if you're on the third or fourth try? What if you're a coward?

"I passed judgment far too soon. As an onlooker, I despised him for fleeing for his life. Those little legs carried him faster than a racing pig. I remember chuckling at that observation behind my armored facemask. It was crass of me, I know, but who's laughing now?

"It's ironic, really, in a morbid sort of way. Though irony is lost in a place like this...so is humor, for that matter.

"If only I weren't so brave, I might still be standing. I challenge my foes head-on, at full speed, and without blinking. The strong are always the first to fight, first to bleed, and first to be mourned. My fans cheered me on, and I had to give them a show worthy of their praise.

"I bit off more than I could chew. Headstrong and overconfident as always. It's been part of my success from an early age. Unfortunately, it was also my downfall this time. I did all I could, and it wasn't enough. Guilt is the dark cousin of regret, and he demands action and offers only death in return." *-Mcgovery, Jousting Champion, age 18.*

Day Two, 7:00 pm: It Starts

Behind his booth table, Kip notices that there is a person lying on the ground.
"He looks hurt."
The continuously blinding brightness makes it almost look to be daytime at night. Then it suddenly becomes quite clear.

"We're under attack!" Kip's voice is blocked by laughter and music from the parade.

Everyone is drinking too much boiled-milk wine to notice or care.

Kip slides over his table in an acrobatic sort of way, jumping into action, knocking over everything on his table in the process. Before he can reach the person on the ground, however, another flash comes, this time right above his district. The sizzling sound is deafening as it arcs through the sky, hitting directly in the middle of the parade route.

Pieces of costumes and people fly every which way as the flash of energy rips through the crowd in an instant. This is no firework or party favor. This is an assault on the castle. The real questions are how and why?

With his mouth agape, Kip is no longer only concerned for the one person on the ground; there are much bigger problems afoot. He is now worried about every last one of them with this overwhelming realization.

Putting his own well-being aside for the moment, Kip tries to get the attention of anyone willing to listen. He frantically grabs the nearest man wearing a proper hat and fancy clothes. From behind, he looks important and influential. Maybe he will help.

The man is currently chatting with a small

group of people with big grins and even bigger drinks.

"You have to find cover, right now! Something isn't right," Kip demands of the man.

"Not you again." The wealthy-looking man pushes Kip to the ground in one simple shove and continues slurring his tale of a hilarious adventure to his group.

"People are getting hurt. Why won't you listen to me?"

"You're interrupting my story during the best part." The wealthy man tosses a of couple coin vouchers, which feather down towards Kip, as if he were barking about the shove.

Shocked, Kip gets up, not giving up. "I don't need your money. I need you to get out of here and help me get others to follow you."

The man puts down his drink on a tall circular table and gets ready to really roughen Kip up for the continuous intrusion.

One of the group members chimes in, "Wait, I think something *is* going on." He points behind Kip at a person fleeing while caught on fire. "That isn't right."

"No, this guy tried to do this to me yesterday," the wealthy man protests, picking Kip off the ground by his leather vest.

With his clothes jammed against his throat, Kip is having a hard time speaking, his feet dangling back and forth looking for solid ground.

Then the man on fire runs into a tent, igniting it ablaze.

This catches the group's attention. "What the..."

The wealthy man releases Kip, causing him to crash into the table, knocking over all the half-drunk and completely empty drinks from their many hours of excess drinking.

Havoc erupts within the group as they all flee in different directions—staggering and veering as if their legs were not up for the task.

Innocent bystanders notice the men running, and like a game of harpy poker, people start to follow suit.

Kip rises to his feet again, rubbing his back where he fell. This is not at all how he imagined being a hero would feel, but he did manage to get the same result in the end, even if it is at the expense of his pride.

While fleeing as well, Kip makes a point to speak with each person in his path. "Find cover if you can!" He tries to warn them about the danger that threatens everyone in the castle. Some listen, others just ignore him completely.

A select few give him a rude hand gesture. One person in particular speaks that gesture aloud. It really is a mixed bag. Whereas some are not so polite and do not express the three virtues of the festival, more are not as rude and do take his warnings to heart.

Kip doesn't have the time to argue with everyone, and sometimes giving up on lost causes is the best course of action. He justifies his guilt as nature's way of culling out the idiotic to save the sounder-mind attendees that follow his stride.

Running through the streets yelling like a madman makes him feel as though he's a cult member warning the world about the impending apocalypse. He has never believed in magic or religion, but the threat of the end of days suddenly seems quite possible, even plausible.

Day Three, 11:28 am: The Taste of Freedom

Staggering out of the castle's kitchen, Kip has forgotten how starved his body really is. Seeing and smelling the chef's meal revitalizes the concept of eating.

The wafting scent of pie unknowingly brings

him across the way to a cookery adjacent to the Taste of All Seasons restaurant. Hungry for survival, he hasn't even thought about having a bite until this moment.

Kip cautiously enters the cookery and finds that no one is there to greet him. Not that he expects a grand tour or anything, but due to the lack of broken glass and furniture, he expected someone to be home. Everything appears to be untouched, as if the place hasn't been ransacked. It seems that he isn't the only person who forgot about meals.

In the display case are day-old breads and pastries.

On the counter is a meaty pie with a perfectly flaky crust—soft, yet buttery.

Before getting permission or thinking things through, Kip indulges in the baked good with both of his unwashed hands. He doesn't care what grime or gore he has on him or what is inside the dish laid out before him, because it's already too late.

Hand over hand, he shoves the still-warm pie into his mouth, enjoying every mesmerizing bite. This has to be the best meal he has ever had in his life, even if he is doing more swallowing than chewing and not savoring the thick, yet juicy, pie.

Kip has a lot of love for the world—for doing the right thing, for succeeding, for making others happy—but never has he ever felt it for an inanimate object. However, in this moment, he truly has found love in its rich flavor.

As fast and hard as it came, it is nearly gone from his life forever. His stomach aches from the sudden shock of hot sustenance to his system.

Being a smaller person, Kip knows he doesn't need to eat it all—at least not *all* right now. Except, he can't help himself. It's far too good, and he is much too starved to show any self-control. Then a thought washes over him, something that he overlooked. *Who made this pie? It was still warm.*

Kip looks around, but no one is here. "Hello?" He looks through the lower and upper cabinets and then goes to the back room, but he still doesn't see anyone around. This place has been deserted. But why? *Maybe they're dead?*

"No. I must stop thinking like that. Everything is going to work out fine. Justice will prevail." Though deep down, Kip knows that everything is far from fine and getting close to complete genocide.

The last couple of hours have been unbearably draining without any respite. He has to think of something to take his mind off the darkness that is taking over his persona. All he wants to do is enjoy his meal, as it might very well be his last one.

Licking his lips and wiping the pie pan clean with his finger, he tries to savor the taste he hurried through. Kip starts to recall the tastes that brought him here in the first place...

It all started with Kip leaving with the jewels of his hometown in the Maelstrom Peaks. Scutter's Landing was the largest city to the south, within several hundred miles, and the best place to fence his goods. But getting there was no easy trip.

In his ancestor's time, the trek was nearly impossible. But a revolutionary traveler known as Bagian Bowler made it all possible with the gift of life. Bagian planted cactus and nut trees along the continental wasteland, creating the great Bagian Road. His path transformed the region for many tribes. It is this very road that brought Kip to Scutter's Landing.

He traveled through harsh colds and crippling heats, through drought and famine.

Snacking on cactus fruits and nuts Bagian left along the way was the only means by which he survived. By the end of it, Kip was an experienced traveler. Still, no map could lead him to the Forgotten Forest.

Only, back then, it was supposed to be found. Kip and his companion Barne—a feathered-folk half-breed—were almost at the end of the line when they stumbled upon a strange place indeed. Kip could only describe it as the inside of a fireplace, what with the burnt-out brush and the ashy surface underfoot.

Barne rubbed his belly, showing his hunger pains.

"I know, me too," Kip said, patting his own stomach in agreement. Without the aid of the Bagian treats, Kip knew they were going to die out there, and his companion wasn't at all helpful.

"Must we walk this way the whole time?" Kip asked, hoping for a change of pace.

"Blind is behind," his companion said with a grin.

Barne had nearly been killed by a blow to the head, and some of his ideas were a little...off. One of which was insisting that they walk backwards everywhere they went.

Kip humored him with this idea, as it might actually throw off some sub-par trackers. Although that wasn't Barne's logic at all, he knew. It was something about turning back time, or that was the gist Kip gathered from his travel companion's ramblings.

It wasn't something that Kip could explain or admit to Barne, but they were most likely going to die out there in the land of death.

Luck is an interesting coin. Just when Kip thought that it had been completely exhausted, the tides of fate turned the benevolent coin to the favorable side.

That is when he saw her—blocking their path.

"Halt human and...abomination," a female voice said from behind them.

If they were walking normally, they might have seen her coming.

Spinning around on his heels, Kip saw a face he never expected to see again...a feathered-folk from the past. Technically, Kip never met her before, but he knew it was her.

"Lancer?"

Upon hearing that name, she quickly got into a fighting stance. "I don't know who you are, but that name dies with you."

Slack-jawed and dumbfounded, Kip was at a loss for words.

With grace and speed, Lancer dashed toward them—ready to strike.

Kip braced for impact with both of his hands protecting his head, but the moment didn't come.

Instead, she stopped dead in her tracks.

Slowly, Kip peeked out from his defensive position.

Lancer's whole demeanor had changed to one that was more inquisitive. "Is that really you?" she asked Barne, who looked back at her with his unique smile.

"It's him," Kip answered for Barne.

Faster than he could comprehend, Lancer spun around him, had her arm wrapped around his neck, and was applying the right amount of pressure to make him miss breathing...and maybe soon living.

"And who might you be?"

Kip tried to respond, but her hold was much too tight on his throat.

"Not so chatty now, are we?" This time she loosened up her grip enough for him to respond.

"I...am a friend."

"I don't need a friend. What I need is a corpse. Are you going to be one of those for me?"

Barne walked up to them both and poked Lancer on the tip of her nose. "Boop."

"What's wrong? What did you do to him?"

"He had an accident."

Lancer released her hold on Kip and walked up to Barne.

"Well then, I can fix him," Lancer said, and just like that, without another word, she led the way.

That was the moment when everything started to go smoothly. Within the next couple of days, she took care of everything—fed them food and water, fought marauders, and even healed Barne's mental state. Just being around her gave Kip a false sense of valor and victory.

Everything was working out better than he ever thought possible. But as quickly as the coin had shifted to his favor, disfavor came back just as wild and even more vengeful than before.

Day Two, 10:40 pm: Getting Closer

The resistance fighters have retreated to a safe clearing behind a large retaining wall.

They made great headway and are taking a beat to deliberate on the best course of survival moving forward. This is no longer a tactical meeting of victory. It is about reducing collateral damage and saving the lives that cannot save themselves. The castle must be evacuated...and fast.

"Everyone, stick to the plan. We need to sweep each area and watch the high ground for sniping spots," Taarl reminds the group.

"How? You know how hard it was to get this far. We lost half our force already. A man with broken armor takes center stage with his claim.

"I'm open for any ideas, if anyone has any," Taarl says, extending out a calming hand. "We just need to keep our heads on straight and keep moving."

"Where are we going to go? It sees everything and everyone."

"I know. Damn it, I know," Taarl says, for the first time losing himself slightly.

"We've gone over this before," the bearded man says, looking like he just walked through hell and back. The hair on top of his head that isn't singed off is matted with blood.

Kip adjusts the helm this man gave him earlier, feeling somewhat guilty.

"We have to be smart about this. There is no stopping that power in the sky. We must stick to the inner castle walls for now until we can find out where it's coming from," one man says, looking out a small slit in the wall used as an arrow window for the time of a normal castle siege. Such a design is completely useless in a situation where the danger is already inside the castle walls.

"What about the arena? We scouted it from afar, and people might indeed be trapped in there," a cloud dancer no bigger than a palm fairy asks, holding a broken arrow as a spear.

"Are you sure about this information?" Taarl asks.

"I've seen it with my own eyes. The doors are closed and locked," a battle-ready woman adds.

"See? Told you. We can ask my brothers and sisters for confirmation, if you desire," the cloud dancer continues.

"Yes, please. If what you say is true, that should be our top priority."

The group gives grunts and nods in agreement to that plan above all else.

The cloud dancer turns into mist and floats out of the arrow-slit window.

"I say we knock down that door," the

bearded man suggests.

"How are we going to go about that exactly? We don't have a battling ram, or any siege weaponry," a thin archer asks while counting his last remaining arrows.

"I will hack it down," the bearded man says matter-of-factly.

"Just get a giant or a cyclops to open it. I'm sure you'll have better odds finding one of those," the archer says sarcastically.

"All you need is a small hole," Kip says, slightly agreeing with the bearded man. "One small enough for people to sneak out one by one."

"Half of them will be dead by the time the other half gets out," the archer challenges.

"It was just a thought," Kip says under his breath, trying to keep optimistic about everything.

Like a bunch of chattering birds, a ruckus of conversation erupts among them. Everyone is talking over each other until they reach a crescendo. This passionate argument reminds Kip of the reunion dinners at his family home.

"Settle down! I think we should just wait for the scout to return with more information. We cannot afford to lose any more people due to unnecessary boldness," Taarl interrupts.

"People are getting killed by the minute, more wounded are dying every hour, and the longer we wait, the more blood is on our hands," a faceless voice says.

Back and forth they argue about the best way to go about tackling this huge obstacle—head-on or stealthily.

Suddenly there is an explosion that causes dust and debris from above to fall on the whole group.

"That was huge. Something is happening." One man runs to the outlook to try to steal a glance.

"Do you see anything?" another man inquires.

Silence falls over the party. The aerial attack has stopped. This is their moment.

"Let's go. Now!" Taarl yells.

Eager to put their preparations to good use, the band of brave men and women rush out of the safety of the inner castle walls, ready to cause retribution on whatever is assaulting their friends, family, and homeland folk.

They are going to take back the castle or die trying. But Kip isn't going with them. He is useless on the front lines due to his crippling fear, which acts as a wall between him and the rest of the group. He takes off down a different path along a dark hallway, doubling back to the people who were left not far behind.

The battlefield is dank, with smoke billowing from the many spot fires still burning—the only source of light in the area. In the aftermath, there is but one touch healer using his arts to stabilize the injured.

Without instruction or command, Kip begins to act as an assistant to the healer by placing wounded people around him in a healing circle.

This is a great opportunity for Kip to help those less fortunate than himself. The wounded are vast and quickly fading into the backs of their eyes. It is up to him to determine the salvageable from the ones past the point of return.

Head wounds, missing limbs, and blood loss are a couple of the only indications he uses in prioritizing who gets immediate attention or not. That about covers the extent of his knowledge of the anatomy of humans and other bloodlines he is inspecting.

One after another, he feels the moistness of the fallens' clothes—if the blood has gone cold, or if they are soaked through, Kip knows that he is much too late and moves on to the next.

"Got one!"

Turning off his thoughts is one of the hardest things he has ever done. Moving without thinking is the only way he can keep up with the task at hand without breaking down completely, giving out under the pressure of the situation.

Back and around, he weaves through the mounds of wounded and dead as he drags a man who is missing a leg towards their central operation. Like a snail, he leaves a trail of red liquid behind marking their roundabout path.

It would be faster and more effective if he would just trample through the fallen, but this isn't his way. He will sacrifice time and his own strength to save people the right way, the way he would want to be saved.

Reaching the triage area, Kip notices a lot more people have come to call. Trained priests, both light and dark, along with many different types of nurses and witchdoctors are now treating the wounded. One greasy-looking man who appears to be dressed like a butcher collects the person Kip brought and starts to dress his wound with a bandage.

He isn't exactly a healer, but he sure knows

how to wrap meat.

Without catching his breath, Kip turns back to get another one.

"Take just a sip," a helper yells at his back to no avail. "You can't go on forever!"

Ignoring the warning, Kip continues with his task.

"Yes, he can...because he has to," an unholy priest says, pulling off his pagan necklace while looking to the ground, his faith forever broken.

And just like that, Kip is at it again, and again, and again. He has never been one for being able to carry even his own weight, but this wounded person was much braver and stronger than Kip in many ways. It's Kip's fortitude, determination, and willpower that are strong, and they carry him through this hope-destroying work.

His muscles ache, his heart hurts heavily, his mind is playing more than just tricks on him, but he doesn't give up. Instead, he gives it all he has left, hoping that is enough.

Two for One

"When will mercy come to call? A wife's tears are not quite wet enough. A child's sulking head isn't tragic enough. Nor is a mother's pain in outliving her kin nearly enough to turn a black heart red again.

"I begged, pleaded, even tried to bribe my way back to the land of the living. Inside his vacant stare, there was nothing there. Humanity had long since gone far, far away.

"I've done a lot of unsavory things in my life. It started at a young age when all I wanted was to prosper. It may have started that way, but I became addicted to the lifestyle—gourmet meals, fancy things and high-priced companionship. Soon that wasn't enough. I tried to kick the habit, but it only took a day or so before I craved the rush. I gave in so easily. One might think I got what I deserved. But you weren't inside my skin when it exploded. No one deserves that. I was too swift and stealthy; he had no way of knowing about my crimes.

"Who knows if, or when, the screams will be granted a benevolent peace. This is the end of happiness, the end of innocence, and possibly the end of existence." -*Fourtoes the Thief, age 15.*

Day Four, 11:45 am: A Helping Hand

All Kip has is the ability to move on. Thinking can cause one to go insane, especially in times like these where nothing makes any sense, where rational thought is obsolete and obscure.

Survival is moving forward, because anything else is giving up, giving in to the end of the world. Especially after seeing people dropping constantly around him—some burning, others cracking, a few much, much worse. The array of things he saw, the frightening images that keep him from moving haunt him with every breath he takes. Only fixating on the objects around him and locking himself out of his mind stops the endless flooding of pain and suffering from consuming him completely.

What can he do to make their deaths not be in vain? They must be something more than an ever-growing number for some maniac god, or whatever is causing this catastrophe to happen.

In a newly opened room, he sees something quite disturbing. Something bad has already come through these parts. There is a large pile of dead bodies, contorted with expressions of pain and horror stuck on their faces.

Kip can't bear to look at them. He tries to reconcile it in his mind, trying to think of them as a pile of food-grade meat instead of people, to dehumanize the event and not think of each person as someone's child, parent, sister, brother, or friend, because doing so is much too hard to fathom.

So much pain can't reasonably be felt by one person in such a short amount of time, especially someone as kind-hearted and compassionate as Kip.

"Turkey legs. A big pile of turkey legs," Kip says, averting his gaze in case reality should prove to betray him at any moment. He needs to rely on his ability to cope, to not dwell on the abyss of despair that is following closely behind him.

Then something familiar catches his eye, outstretched from the meat pile. He doesn't want to get any closer than he needs to, but it is the very reason he came to this event in the first place, to be selfless and do good.

His heart has already broken; what's one more crack among his infinite defeat?

He cannot stop himself any more than he can pretend this isn't happening. Kip falls to his knees and into a death clutch, desperately holding on to the very reason he is here...

Day One, 8:17 am: Familiar Face

Before he can shake off the uncomfortable situation at the registration table, Kip is stopped in the street by another vendor he had met in previous years. "Kippy! Glad to see you back. Where's your partner?"

"Oh, hello, Chani!" Kip greets the man who is pushing a cart filled with every fur, scale, and skin imaginable. "He's been busy traveling and couldn't get out this year. In life, you have to take advantage of your blessings and not take them for granted. That would be a slap in the face of those less fortunate than you."

"Hey, I hear you. You have to do what you will while you still can," Chani says, tapping a stick against his wooden leg, which is hidden from view under his fur-lined pants.

This isn't exactly what Kip meant, but he accepts the sentiment all the same.

"Which reminds me, I have a couple for you this year. They just fell into my lap, literally. I was so excited when I found them."

"Splendid! That *is* very exciting," Kip says with a great big smile on his face. He struggles to find a free hand, and nearly all his signs, bags, and everything else come crashing down.

"Oh, hey, watch out. Don't get too excited."

"Great. So great! Even finding one makes this whole trip worth the effort."

"That look, that's that look I've been waiting for. When I found them, I just thought about how happy it would make you."

Kip feels flush all of a sudden, he never noticed how apparent his emotions are to others. He really does wear his heart on his sleeve. When you have nothing foul inside, you have nothing to fear in giving away too much of yourself to others. "This is the year. Our quest is almost complete."

"You said that last year, but I'm rooting for

you, buddy. Make sure you come by the booth later, and I'll give them to you then."

"I feel like this year is going to be different somehow. Call it gypsy science or mother's intuition, but I just know it somehow."

"Most definitely. I just want to say, it's a wonderful thing that you guys are doing here...real heroes' work."

"Nah. It's the right thing to do—what anyone would do in our situation."

"I don't know about that," Chani says, slightly cringing at the pile of carcass hides in his own cart. "But good on you two. Really inspiring stuff." Chani pats Kip on the side of his shoulder.

"Say, do you need any help with that stuff? If you want, you can put your load on my cart, and I can take it to your spot in a bit."

"It's okay. A little manual labor is good for me."

"Suit yourself. Let's meet up later, yeah?"

With a heart-felt nod and a wave, Chani pushes his cart past Kip in the direction of the registration booth.

Kip wants to warn his friend about the registration lady, or at the very least say some clever quip about it, but Chani is already out of earshot. Yelling at this point might make Kip seem like the crazy one. With his mouth drying out and his tired arms full of gear, Kip falls flat on his words. Instead, Kip gives Chani a nod that he doesn't see.

Day Four, 11:50 am: The Gift

One by one, Kip pulls back the fingers clutching on to the gift that Chani had for him all along—two glorious feathered-folk pits. Even in death, Chani knew the importance of such artifacts and what it meant to Kip to find them.

Hundreds of forest folk had already been relocated in hopes of finding new lands and a chance at a reincarnation. The secret lies in their pits—the only part of them left behind after their deaths. This is the real reason Kip's partner is traveling so much—he is trying to find a new forest for his people to call home.

Kip's heart sinks as it is abundantly clear that Chani was on his way to Kip's booth when the disaster struck. Instead of saving himself, he must have been trying to give the gift that was promised. *How could he be so selflessly bold in such a time of peril?* Kip turns away, not wanting to see his friend in agony under this giant pile of turkey.

"For you, good friend." Kip decides to overcome his own fears and truly look at the pile of meat in front of him, because to ignore it is to act as if it never happened.

In no world does he want to live where this sort of murder is the new normal. Each life is a travesty that needs to be remembered and mourned separately.

Men and women, tall and small, old and young. Humans, people of the sky, orcas, grounders, and beastlings. No matter their tribe, origin or creed, each one is a unique being, beautiful and tragic; and their life ended far too soon, far too young, no matter their age. Kip thanks each one, burning their visages into his mind to remember always. It takes a little rummaging, but no soul will be lost among the lot. For they are resting here so that he may continue on—others can live on.

"You all gave your lives so that these two could be reborn," Kips says, choked up. "I only wish there were something I could do for you in return." With a gentle nod, he holds up the two feathered-folk pits before placing them back in his pack. "As the wind blows and the sky cries, I will breathe life into your sacrifice."

Kips eyes become blurry as he faces his fears with trembling lips. This is not the end of it all. This is just the beginning of the fight.

Getting up Again

"Selfishness is a chore reserved desperately for the unmotivated. Laziness often leads to cutting corners and drawing blood with the sharp corners of their cruelty.

"I took life for granted. Ate far past the point of getting full. But why not? My opulence allows me to do so. I am no champion, and I haven't a need to fit into any armor. A suit for me would cost twice as much as a normal man's in materials alone. Besides, those things are hot, and I have always been prone to sweating. No, best leave the warrioring to the warriors. Just by looking at me, you know what I'm good at. I don't begin to try and hide it.

"Maybe I could have tried to run, but I

wouldn't have gotten very far, not in my condition. So, with a napkin delicately draped on my lap, I watched the show unfold while finishing my meal. I was far from hungry, but this turkey leg was the best I'd ever had, and I thought putting it to waste was a crime worse than death.

"I am always the first to admit when I am wrong. I know now that there is no fate worse than death. My troubles didn't just happen. They were years and years in the making. I'd been weighing myself down until I had finally become too encumbered to move.

"I sipped the last bit of wine out of my silver goblet and dabbed my mouth dry. It is easy to be a barbarian. It takes a real gentleman to remain civilized." *-Duke Rowen, age 47.*

Day Three, 2:14 am: Fish in a Barrel

Without reinforcements, Kip makes his way down the long stretch of steps around the bend. With each passing step, he finds himself closer to danger than he would have hoped.

For the first time since this whole thing started, the sky is pitch black, without a speckled star in sight. Something has most assuredly changed in the late hours of the night.

It is very quiet in this part of the castle. In the distance, he can still hear the battle taking place on the far side of the courtyard.

Sounds of destruction pound throughout the night's sky. There is no way for him to know which side is winning, or if there even are sides.

Kip makes his way to the clearing that spills out into the front section of the arena. This is where the warriors are trying to reach.

Hundreds of hands and feet are tapping, banging, and kicking against the inner side of the steel-reinforced wooden walls surrounding the stadium seating. People are trapped in there.

"Hello? Can you hear me?" Kip yells through the gaps between wooden slats, hoping to reach whoever is on the other side.

Muffled cries of desperation and even more banging respond to his call.

"What do you need me to do? How can I help you get out of there?" Kip asks, though his words don't seem to produce any different re-action. It's all just more banging and hysterics.

No amount of Kip's pitiful pulling is going to make the slightest bit of difference in opening this massive door. The arena was built to double as a stronghold if ever the castle was under siege. It does no good if the threat is coming from inside the very place made to hunker down in.

Poor design or not, people are trapped in there, and there is nothing Kip can do to open up the entrance.

Things suddenly get really quiet. It is both eerie and chilling. To Kip, it feels as though time has frozen over. He fears the worst must have happened to the people he desperately wants to save.

"Hello? Is anyone still in there? Please say something." His voice has no echo and sounds dead like the night.

Frantic, Kip looks around for something he can use, but there is nothing. Everything is broken beyond repair.

"I am sick and tired of being so useless!" Kip bangs his fist against his forehead in frustration.

Then he hears a faint sound.

"What was that? I can't hear you. Speak up, please. Are you alright?" Hope is tickling at his sanity.

"Get away from the doors!" the voice says again, louder this time.

Without looking back, Kip runs for his life.

One thing that he has learned as of late is if someone tells you to run, you don't ask any questions.

A series of explosions goes off behind the doors, blowing the hinges clean off.

Running for his life, Kip barely manages to get out of the way of the falling steel-reinforced doors that come crashing down like a meteor.

The gust of wind the doors make when they touch down picks Kip up a couple feet in the air.

Flailing around, he falls to the ground with a hard thud.

Then the rumbling sound of stamping feet follows. People trample over each other trying to get away from whatever is inside, and they are coming straight for him.

Day One, 10:59 am: Flood Gates

Excitement for the day overtakes Kip's nerves as he watches his hands shake violently in anticipation. There is a lot at stake here, and it isn't at all about his own personal livelihood. It's about helping others.

This is his first time manning the booth alone and without his partner. Kip has to worry about sales, marketing, and now thieves, apparently. He gently pats the dagger stowed at his hip, thinking of the latter concern. Among all the little details floating around in his brain, he still hasn't figured out his meal plans and bathroom breaks, or just normal breaks for that matter. There is so much for him to consider, and no time left to prepare for any of it. Leaving the booth could result in the loss of a sale, and he can't pack up his stuff every time nature calls. His only option is to make friends with another vendor in the hopes that they can safely watch each other's wares while the other takes a break.

Unfortunately, his neighbor to the left, Sarl, seems odd and not at all interested in getting to know Kip. And at this point, the feeling is mutual.

However, first impressions can be tough because you have no pattern to hold the single encounter up to. There is no way to know what the other person is going through; did someone close to them pass? Or maybe they have a headache. Sometimes you can just catch somebody at the wrong place at the wrong time.

After talking to a couple of merchants this morning, apparently it is a little-known fact that vendor-on-vendor crime is not uncommon at an event such as this, especially when sales are lower than expected. Still, the fact that it happened before the festivities even began is what strikes him as strange.

After calming down, Kip decides that he was too haste in his judgment. Maybe later on he will have to try and work things out with Sarl, if his bladder has anything to say about it. If that doesn't turn out, he can always talk to the eccentric-looking female vendors across the way.

No. On second thought, Sarl will have to do. Talking to girls is troublesome.

The loud unraveling sound of metal chains against a cog echoes throughout the kingdom. It must be the castle's drawbridge. Dutiful horns blow from trumpeters' lips. The ceremony has begun. There is no going back.

Once the drawbridge falls in place with a thunderous boom, a seemingly endless sea of people fills the grounds in an orderly fashion. After about fifteen minutes, the mob finally makes their way to the bargaining district where Kip is located.

Wide-eyed and heavy-pocketed, everyone is eager to see what this year's festival has to offer.

Kip stumbles around making sure his display is just right, though deep down he knows that the first of couple hours are really just for browsing. People always want to make their first round before settling on any purchases.

Travelers come from all walks of life and levels of wealth. Some of the poorer folks might only have enough vouchers to buy one item for the whole week. These types are Kip's bread and butter. He has an opportunity for them to pick up some easy vouchers and allow them to afford many more souvenirs if they're willing to put in a little legwork.

Never has Kip seen so many attendees for the annual event. They just keep coming with no end in sight. He knows for certain that this is going to be the best year ever.

Day Three, 2:26 am: Against the Tide

Pushing forward, Kip fights against the mass of people fleeing from the fallen arena doors. Fire and smoke are bursting whence they come. Something is going on inside. Something is fighting the threat and keeping the pulses at bay, but also giving the people an opening to escape through.

Kip can only hope that the adventurers have made it safely inside in his absence.

Left and right, people are running out of control towards him, elbowing and shoving anyone who happens to be standing in their way. Havoc ensues in the danger of the night.

This is not how he views the moral compass of his fellow people. Sure, humans often get a bad rap for a lot of things, but there were forest folk, undermen, and even grounders among them.

Stay calm and collected. Kip knows that the first thing to do in any crisis is to let the shock wear off. Then you will be able stop all your rash decisions and can start to think clearly. But they're all acting in such a selfish manner. "Everyone, calm down," he yells, trying to put some order to the confusion and mass hysteria that is going on.

In the center of the stampede stands an elderly woman. She looks to be silently screaming at the top of her lungs, but her voice is masked by the ruckus of the crowd. She seems tranquil and silent, as if under water. Her hair flows slowly against the frenzy. Somehow, she reminds him of his mother, and he just has to save her. He has to do something to squelch that silent scream of hers.

Kip tries to muscle his way over to her to see

what is the matter, though he is no match for the opposing traffic, as the congestion of people builds. Especially when the dense mob is fueled with adrenaline. They all seem to have super human-like strength.

A man holding his glass eye in between his fingers shoves a priest to the ground without thinking twice about it.

Kip pushes his way towards him. "We need to work together. No one is going to survive by being divided," he says, extending a helpful hand.

The priest quickly takes his gesture and pulls himself up. In turn, his actions knock Kip to the ground instead. On his way out, the priest steps on Kip's leg as he flees for his own life.

This isn't very religious for a man of the cloth.

"Ouch. Are you kidding me?" Kip looks around, though no one is so foolish as to come to his aid in the same way that he just did for the priest. He wonders if he's the only one left who has any decency left in the world. Getting kicked, stepped on, and completely ignored doesn't help his wonder any. At the beginning of the convention, every attendee seemed to be happy and quite goodly. But that was only on the surface—a façade. Back then, it wasn't a life-or-death situation, and no one had to prove their worth to anything or anyone.

Early on in his life, Kip knew that saving someone was going to be his downfall. It has always been woven into his soul. No matter the situation, he just can't live with throwing someone to the wolves in order to save his own meat and bones. Only there is no one willing to do the same for him. So, he must save himself to the best of his ability.

Like a cockroach, he dodges and rolls out of the way of the relentlessly stomping feet. In this instance, his small frame is proving quite helpful—just barely getting him out of harm's way.

Kip catches his breath at the edge of an upheaved cart. *They deserve what's coming to them.* "No, no. They're just scared and not thinking clearly." He shakes off the notion that almost breaks his spirit.

He has to get back in there, back to helping the party of heroes. Kip starts going against the grain, without concern for his own safety. All he sees is the whites of their wide eyes and the terror displayed on their appalled faces. They are not thinking. They are motivated by instincts alone, like a bunch of grass eaters fleeing from a predatory animal.

Suddenly a man in the crowd trips over himself and face-plants on the ground. Like the priest and the old woman, no one stops to help. Only this time, they use him as a stepping stone—trampling him into the hard cobblestone ground.

"You're killing him!" Kip shoves people as he tries to reach the man in time, fighting the opposing forces in play.

His cry lands on deaf ears. No one cares; no one is going to care. This is madness, and he is stuck in the heart of it. This could have been him. In fact, this was him only moments ago.

More people fall to the left of him and the right. He can't do anything to help them, nor to stop the crowd. He cannot watch this level of brutality.

"Get out of the way, runt!" one fleeing man says, pushing Kip to the side like an object rather than a person. Kip starts to lose his balance slightly. His movements are not his own as he is tossed around like a ragdoll.

This is not good. There are many more people in this small, confined corridor than there were a little bit ago. There is no more room for him to roll his way out this time. He starts to fall to the ground. The world around him grows darker from the shadows of the people. He is almost at leg level when he grabs ahold of someone's backpack.

No longer able to tell where the hits are coming from, his whole body is numb in the pit of raging people as he is dragged behind the owner of the backpack.

Who knows how many people were trapped in the event hall. It must have been full. With such a small opening, everyone is bottlenecking through this one exit, and there is no other way around it.

He proceeds to be pushed along with the current of people. The backpack is his only saving grace, and he holds on for dear life.

Kip looks back trying to spy the old woman, but she is lost in the crowd. He wants to go back to help her the first chance he gets. The only thing about chances is that they don't always materialize when you need them to.

When a Feeling Stands Still

"When life falls apart, it's the pieces that need to be found in order to make any sense of the madness that's puzzling you. My goal wasn't to stop it. I only wanted to study and observe. This was all in order to understand what was going on from a purely speculative standpoint. It is like taking out the insides of an animal to better know yourself. What was once thought of as insanity can become sane by understanding the motivation.

"Admiration does not strictly mean that you condone the actions. Respect is unbiased when it comes to these types of things. From the shadows of the destruction, I wrote in my journal every blasted thought and observation. Using my own blood as ink, I scratched down even things no words could describe. Instead, I let my tears tell the story against red ink.

"This was my life's work. It's the only thing I've ever written that meant something, not for the execution or style of my writing, but because it had never been done before. I did my best with every drop I had left...until I ran dry. Someday, somewhere, someone will find my notes, and when they do, I too will be undone.

"When deep in the face of adversity, you can hold your breath or bite its wicked nose clean off." *-Zarls the Scribe, age 14.*

Day Three, 6:42 pm: Into the Dark

With interlocked hands, Kip and the bride, whose name he forgot to ask, race through dank cobblestone streets, looking for refuge. His free hand is holding a thick fur-lined fabric, which he plans on hiding under if something inexplicable happens again.

"This looks promising," Kip says as they walk down a street filled with still erect residential housing.

Kip tries to release himself from her grip to knock on the first door to their left, but she only holds on tighter.

"No. I don't want to risk getting separated," she says, pulling him in closer to her.

"Okay. Then can you knock?" he asks, looking down at his baggage filling his other arm.

She reaches out and holds a closed fist up to the door, but that is it.

"Go on. It's okay."

"Are you sure?" She gives him a hesitant gaze.

"People want to help. If there is someone there, they'll come to our aid. You just have to believe."

"I like how you think." A shimmer comes to her eyes and a slight upturn of her lips. "Okay."

Quick and polite, she gives three nice little knocks. They are cute and courteous.

Kip feels her grip tighten as the excitement grows. Her hands are so soft and dainty, but he knows her nails are both sharp and deadly.

They both wait in anticipation, but nothing happens.

"We should go," she says, loosening her grip.

"Try one more time."

"I..."

The warm light that was shining through the

upstairs window suddenly turns dark.

"That is uncalled for," Kip says, looking up.

With a slight tug on his arm, she says, "Let's go."

"No. That is just rude. I can see you up there. Lanterns don't just turn themselves off, you know. If I weren't such a good person, I might see that as an opportunity to rob you or hold you hostage," Kip rants just loud enough to make sure the person inside can hear him.

"Come on."

Kip doesn't like showing her his disappointed side. It is a feeling he has to fight constantly to try and keep himself motivated. But as of late, it seems to be the one beating him down.

"Hold on." Kip tries to place the blanket on his back so that he can sort out this misunderstanding.

She shakes her head "no" with a sadness coming over her once more. It is a look that nearly cripples him.

With the reinforced toes of his borrowed boots, he gives the door three hard kicks. Boom, boom, boom. "This is how you deal with people like this."

She doesn't have to say a word. He knows

how she's feeling through her touch. Her fingers, they're twitching.

The door flies open, and the sharp end of an arrow points outward. Two beady eyes stare them both down.

Kip suddenly changes his tune. "Excuse me, I…"

"You're bringing it here. Die someplace else," the figure shrouded in the darkness of the doorway says.

The bride points to the intersecting street. Her hands are now trembling.

"We just wanted to…" Kip turns to see what the arrow is actually pointing at.

A long shadow creeps across the stone floor and up the wall. It consumes everything it touches as it makes its approach. This is different than the fog. This thing is alive.

It moves unnaturally, and as far as Kip can tell, it isn't attached to anything substantial.

"Run!" Kip commands.

Across their backs, arrow after arrow takes flight towards whatever is at their heels.

Running for their lives, Kip and the girl stop at each doorway on their way down the street—frantically banging on them.

"Get out. It's coming."

"Save yourself."

"There is no time.

"Don't let us in. Let yourself out."

They try to warn people, but it is no use. Everyone is too scared to move.

A torturing scream of agony from behind keeps them moving.

"Why aren't they listening?" the bride asks, as they reach the dead end of the street.

"They're scared."

"Well, so am I," she admits.

But Kip already knows that. Standing protectively in front of her, holding her hand behind him, Kip bravely says, "Don't you worry. I am going to protect you," although Kip doesn't know exactly how he is going to succeed in his assertion.

He is looking death directly in the face. The darkness is crawling from one building to the next, consuming all that life and light have to offer.

Terrible sounds echo out of each broken door as the darkness slowly makes its way towards Kip and the woman.

"You don't have to be brave."

"What?" This catches Kip off guard. All he ever wants to be is bigger, stronger, and braver.

"For me. You don't have to be brave for me. I like you anyway," she says, nuzzling up to the back of his neck.

"But..." he starts to say but then pauses, not wanting to ruin the moment with him overthinking it, "...you're married."

"No, I'm a widow." She tickles his neck with her nose.

This changes everything. Being brave has always been very hard for Kip, but running and hiding comes quite naturally.

His eyes dart back and forth for an alternative option.

Then he sees it—a storm drain leading to the sewers. "There!" Kip points, and together they rush towards it.

"I don't know if I can fit down there," the woman says.

"You have to." Kip tries to help her on her belly and guides her backwards down the hole. She still won't let go of his hand. He has learned not to push that point any longer. She is going to hold on for dear life no matter what.

"It smells strange down here, and it is pitch black."

"Exactly. That is why it won't follow us. It's after the light."

She's safe inside. Nothing but her hand remains in view.

The living darkness sees him, and it has just finished destroying the last building on the block.

Kip stares at the evil that draws near. In this moment he sees it for what it is...hungry.

Deep inside himself, he feels a power building up. Whatever it is, he isn't scared. Not of the darkness, not of death, not of anything.

"Hurry up," she says with a squeal, snapping him out himself.

The darkness charges at him, manifesting as a horrid monster of a thing.

The woman pulls him into the sewer, and the lamppost outside goes dark...along with everything else.

***

Walking aimlessly in the pitch black under the city, Kip feels a shiver escape her cold hand.

"Hold on."

Neither of them can see a thing and are reduced to relying on their sense of touch for everything.

"What's wrong? Why are we stopping?"

His cheek brushes up against hers as he fumbles around with the fur fabric he is holding. Distracted, he breathes in deeply. The tiny peach fuzz on her skin reaches for his inhalation. Her aroma matches her personality perfectly—adorably sweet.

A couple of twist and turns later and he manages to wrap the fur fabric around her completely without letting go of her hand.

"Oh, you didn't have to."

"Is that better?"

He feels her body contract into the fur as she snuggles into it.

"Oh, good," Kip says, taking her action as a response.

He caresses her hand with his to encourage them onward. Time drifts on the ocean of sand toward a new moment.

Sharing the blackness together, everything is still and slow. No longer can they hear the misery of the struggle outside.

As if marching, they walk in unison. Their echoing footfalls sound as though only one person is about. They're in tune with each other. When one inhales, the other exhales, almost as if they're breathing each other in.

In this dark world they have built with each

other, nothing exists beyond their beating hearts and bated breaths.

Day Two, 8:50 pm: This is Not Happening

K ip is face-down in the open crowd. Many different sounds from this massive execution shatter throughout the area. First, there is a *whoosh* sensation that makes him feel whole, followed by a sound that resembles a burning map being crumpled into a ball. There is also something Kip thinks of as an implosion—the point where everyone turns inside out. It is a moist, wet feeling that churns your stomach upside down.

There is also the surge of electricity that he first saw snake through the sky, which he mistakenly thought was part of the event's theatrics. The last attack that he can recognize among the foreign sounds is a haunting noise. It has a low rumbling effect that seems to be coming out of the darkness itself.

As far as he can tell, there are nine or ten distinct attacks that are going on at once from all different directions—some overlapping, others not so much. This must mean that there are at least that many squadrons afoot.

Using his fingers to tap out patterns in the sounds, Kip tries to determine their unique signatures to hopefully shed some light on to what exactly is going on. If he can understand it, maybe he can beat it, or at least beat letting it get him.

This is not a military castle. It is used for personal occupancy. What gain would there be for anyone to attack such a place, Kip ponders to himself silently. Nothing about this situation makes any sense. It is almost as if it had been planned out solely for maximum devastation. The only people who would have a motive to carry out such an assault would be the very people Kip has dedicated his life to save—the feathered folk. *But that is impossible.* Kip quickly tosses out that notion. *This is not their way. Besides, how could anyone do such a thing?*

His mind feels as though it is breaking trying to solve this riddle without gleaning any new information. The only acceptable answer he can think of is something that is untrue. "It must be a demon or demonic deity." Nothing else seems to add up to him. This conclusion gives him the justification to stay put. "I mean, how can I expect to compete with that?"

All he can do is sit and listen to the horrifying sounds until he gains control over his courage again.

"Run...quick. People are getting hurt," a voice says among the horror.

Zap...zap...zap...zap...

"I can't feel my wrists. I can see them, but it is like they're not there," someone else cries out.

So many people are talking over each other, it is hard to determine what is happening and to whom.

Rat-a-tat-tat-tat-tat...

"Ouch. I'm hit."

"Get off me. You're crushing me."

Brawn...brawn...brawn...zeurppp

"It's for your safety, my dearest darling."

"Find cover!"

"Get out of the open."

"Come here. It's safe. Hurry, Bae."

Projectiles and debris zoom above their heads, slicing through the air, and bouncing off of anything that isn't soft enough for them to get lodged into.

"Where is it coming from?"

"Everywhere!"

Rat-a-tat-tat-tat-tat...

"People are dying...People are..."

Splat...splat...crash...

"We have to get out of here before we get trapped!"

"I told you the end was coming, muhaha."

"Shut up already."

"I am missing my child. Where is my child? Someone please..."

Brawn...brawn...brawn...zeurppp

"I lead a good life. I am going to make a run for it. I should be fine."

"Get back here. You're going the wrong way!"

"Oh no, it got him. He's down..."

"Is someone going to help that nice man?"

"Go ahead, get yourself killed."

"I can't, my elbow is broken."

"Nice excuse."

"We are sitting ducks. This is a coward's fight."

Rat-a-tat-tat-tat-tat...

"It isn't safe on the ground. Something just got me!"

Upon hearing these words of terror, Kip takes to his legs and runs towards an abandoned artisan's stage, seeking refuge. There are plenty of props and cover to hide behind. A couple of other people follow his lead.

On the first day, Kip remembers briefly watching a performance there. He distinctly recalls an actor disappearing through a trap door during the second act. This could be his ticket out of here—if only a temporary one.

Racing along in his sure-footed sprint, there are a lot of large lumps he has to avoid. He doesn't know if it's debris or people, nor does he care at this time. Sure, in general he does, but currently he feels as though he's in a daze—not really alive, nor dead. It is as if he's in a moment between the two worlds.

A person next to him gets struck by some force and tumbles to the ground violently. Instead of stopping and helping, like how he was taught to do ever since childhood, he keeps his eyes fixated on his destination. One by one, fleeing people are dropping all around him, and he keeps his glassy-eyed stare forward.

Don't look away. Don't look away.

Without glancing at them, he can trick himself into believing that they are just props, like stage actors playing a part, and not in fact dying people to the left and right of him.

Something zooms by his brow, nearly

stopping him in his tracks.

This is a bad idea.

With his chest heaving up and down, starving for oxygen, he gains a sudden clarity. *This is an ambush. Whatever is out there is preying on the fleeing people, and everyone is falling right into the trap.* There is no way he is ever going to make it to the trap door in time.

"It's a trick. Follow me. This way!" Kip turns on his heels in the opposite direction, now running towards the source of the danger.

The more he runs, the more he knows his observation is spot on. The fleeing people have no chance of survival. They never did.

Going against the herd, he spots a light in the distance giving notice to the trajectory of the attack. It is only a slight advantage, but anything is better than nothing when the difference between life and death is the distance between a couple of hairs.

Why won't they listen to me? He has to save himself, just as everyone else has to try and do the same. Only time can judge who has the better plan of survival.

Day Four, 9:14 am: Survivors

Kip limps through the desolate street with his head held low, no longer clamoring for heroics like a fool. Soot covers his body as a reminder of the morning's pain.

He looks down at his bandaged hands. "What is the point of putting yourself out there if an end is all that is waiting for you?"

He tried—so many times has he tried—and with each end result comes another devastation he wishes he hadn't witnessed.

Close by, he hears the sound of something shattering.

"Psst, anyone out there?" Kip says to a pile of broken games, where you could normally play for a chance to win prizes. Torn-up dolls and headless stuffed animals are spread around the ground.

He continues looking for someone who might be still about. "This isn't a trick. I wish only to help."

Still there is no answer. He wonders if maybe he is the last one left around. Since the stable girl, he hasn't seen a living soul.

Spots of red are scattered throughout the atrium, each one representing another life lost. They're all different sizes. Some are blending together. It is impossible to count how many lives were lost in this spot alone.

"It is safe to come out...right now, anyway. Please listen to me." Since the firefight, things are reasonably quiet in this area.

"Go away," a voice echoes softly.

"Hello? Where are you?" Kip sees this as an opportunity to redeem himself.

"..."

Kip walks over to a broken fountain. Inside it is filled with shattered statue parts—a shoulder, a hand, some unrecognizable pieces of stone. His stomach lurches at the sight, reminding him of a very similar scene he saw the night before involving real people being destroyed in a similar way.

A slight ripple in the water alerts him to a small hiding place half in the water, half under a stone fairy.

"That is a very clever spot," Kip says to the two little eyes peering out at him.

"I said leave me be," the voice responds through chattering teeth.

"It seems safe to come out now," Kip says, trying to muster a fake encouraging smile, though he has no reason to be happy. This is a dark day filled with loss.

"I don't believe you. How can you be so

sure?"

"Look. I am alive. A little banged up, but still breathing."

"It's a trick!" another voice says from across the way.

"Will you just trust me. It will be okay. I give you my word." Even through all of this madness, there is one thing Kip holds on to that is dearest. It's his word. He never intentionally breaks his word once given. Likewise, he doesn't make promises beyond his control. To him, this seems like a safe bet.

After a long moment, the first kid makes his way to meet Kip. Water droplets almost hide the tears rolling down his cheeks.

One by one, children start coming out of their little hiding holes. Dozens of them were practically in plain sight, using their small bodies to fit places no normal-sized person could.

"There you go. See? Let's try and work together and get out of here."

"Okay," says a dirt-smeared adolescent boy.

Kip hopes that none of these youths saw a fraction of the things he did. If they had, he cannot imagine them living normal, well-adjusted lives.

The group forms around Kip, with one

exhausted child on his back. Their tired eyes are eager for direction. Maybe it is an excuse to see her again, or maybe he knows it is the safest place he has found, but he plans on taking them to the sewers.

"This way, everyone."

Out of the shadows that the children cast, powerful dark energy blobs fly out rapidly in all directions.

"Run!" a chubby kid yells.

The evil is literally underfoot.

Everyone starts to scatter like roaches in the candlelight.

Random kids are getting hit by the dark orbs, dropping them to the floor.

This is not what Kip had in mind. It is a trap, one that Kip unwittingly helped spring. He can't understand...why hadn't that happened when he was walking alone?

A huge rumbling sound shakes the cobblestones below him. The kid on his back kicks him in the side like a horse.

Kip clutches his side in pain.

Tears of remorse are the only movement on Kip's paralyzed body. He wants to help them, to call out to them to make amends, but his fear won't let him. It is as if he is reverting back to his own inner child. He should have let them be, left them to fend for themselves.

"To the basement," the eldest-looking one yells, smashing opening a door leading to the underground belly of the castle, but not to the sewers.

Where Kip has failed, someone younger steps up. Kip cannot help but feel horrible that this kid is not even a teenager, and he is already more heroic than him.

The leading teen grabs the kid off Kip's back and drops him off at the entrance of the stair-well.

As each child leaves the outside world for the dark stairwell, one less shadow with shooting orbs is cast.

Finally, the kid in the fountain is the last one who remains.

"Run faster!" the teen commands, with an outstretched hand.

Inbound is the last dark blob, and it's in line to hit the wet fellow.

Without hesitation, the teen stands in front of the fountain kid using his body as a shield from the loose projectile.

He takes a hit head-on then falls over life-less, smoke pouring out of the hole the dark blob has made.

Suddenly Kip has found his legs again and runs to aid them both. Pulling off the teen, the fountain kid immediately starts to slap and kick Kip with all his hatred. "You said it was safe. You promised us that it would be okay."

"I know. I am so, so, sorry. I thought..."

"You are a bad man. You are a really bad man!"

"Please let me make it up to you."

"You can't ever bring him back. He was my brother. He was all I had in this world, and you took him from me."

"I wanted to help. I just froze. You have to believe me."

Even though it hurts a lot, each kick and slap the kid distributes on Kip can't possibly take away the pain he feels in his heart for what he has done.

"It doesn't matter. Nothing matters," the kid begins to sob.

"Yes, it does. Life has to matter, or else why were you hiding in the first place?"

"I want to die with my brother."

"Don't say that. He gave his life for you. Don't make his sacrifice in vain."

For a moment, the kid stops fighting Kip to

wipe away his tears, but they keep streaking down his face.

Kip doesn't know if his words are reaching him or if the kid has stopped from exhaustion. In either case, he has to do something.

Grabbing the kid by the scruff of his shirt, Kip heads to the underground, dragging the kid behind him—kicking and flailing away.

Fire with Firepower

"To give yourself for another is a power that can never be stolen, a sacrifice that will always be remembered, a gift that will never be taken for granted.

"There are a great many things I've never seen or done. Attending the festival was an adventure in itself. At least it was for me. I stick close to home and mostly keep to myself. I never wanted to be a hermit; I just get dreadfully awkward in the face of others. I assure you, when I am alone and in the comfort of my own things, I am quite chatty. I have many great ideas and inspiring views on the world. My wit is unparalleled, I do say so myself. But I wouldn't say anything if someone else was around because I lose my voice. Why can't I just be normal? Everyone else is reacting to this thing in a normal sort of way. Why can't I join in their screams? Even now, nothing comes out. Do they notice me acting so weird? People would love me if I only knew how to open myself up to them. I need to let them give me a chance.

"In the heat of the moment, the surge of the battle, one person saw me. Without words, I used my body to protect them. She really saw me for what I was—a hero. And for the first, and last, time it felt natural. This is by far the best honeymoon I could have asked for." -*Palic the Hero, age 36.*

Day One, 8:41 am: The Neighbor

*K*ip makes his way to the rented booth which will serve as his temporary shop for the entire week. Unfortunately, it seems as though whoever constructed his spot didn't put enough effort into making sure it would last the entirety of the show. The legs are wobbly, and there is a rotted spot in the middle of the table. He wants to complain to the management, but that isn't his way. He will have to make do with what was given to him.

A long-winded sigh escapes out while he struggles to cover the scratchy wood with some cloth. The rough wood is sticking through and ripping his fabric in many different places.

"I give up," Kip says after getting a third splinter in his hand.

He moves on to placing his signs and banners. "Pits and Seeds, Plants and Weeds," is what his sign reads. This is one of his marketing schemes to attract a certain type of clientele. Even though he only has a handful of plants for sale, they are more a cover for his real intent. If he didn't have any merchandise to sell, they wouldn't exactly let him set up for the show. So, he plays the part of a traveling merchant—one who doesn't even have enough product to cover his table costs. But that isn't a concern for Kip.

Only a few select people know the truth behind his deception. There is no ill intent for this cover. This isn't some undercover arms deal, or illegal animal trade, or worse. He is on the side of valor and righteousness, or so he believes. In the grand scheme of things, isn't everyone in their own right?

"Sometimes a hero must lie about being a prince to save a princess," Kip says under his breath as he prepares himself to embark on the day.

After reinforcing his table with some scrap wood he found, his booth neighbor—a gruff man with a strong jaw and tanned skin—arrives at the spot next to Kip.

"Greetings, I'm Kip. Is this your first year?" His cheerfulness doesn't seem to go over well, as the man gives him a scowl.

After looking Kip up and down, he finally responds, "The name's Sarl—blasting supplies and fire accessories."

Kip's eyes light up and his mouth hangs open, but before he can say anything, the neighbor interrupts him with a nonchalant hand gesture.

"Yes, this is my first time," Sarl continues.

"I've been here since the very first one. You can ask me anything. I don't mind." After a beat of silence, Kip fully regrets his comment. He doesn't know what he said, but his words somehow have stopped the conversation dead in its tracks.

As if they weren't even talking, Sarl pulls out bag after colorful bag of product, stacking them on his table. There are crates and crates of the stuff. It's a real contrast to what Kip brought, which is only a handful of plants on and around his table. If anyone were to look under his tablecloth, they would see that what is out just about covers the full extent of his full inventory.

After many long moments of silence, Kip notices his neighbor struggling with a heavy crate he is trying to stack three-high.

"Need a hand?" Kip rushes over before Sarl has a chance to reject him. They are going to be spending a lot of time in close proximity to each other, and Kip doesn't want it to be any more awkward than it already is.

"Wait. Careful with that stuff. It's explosive," Sarl barks back.

"Explosive," Kip queries, nearly dropping the crate.

"Yes, it's a blasting supply, like I said before."

"Right..." Kip doesn't quite understand how they are relevant here at the festival. "Explosives?"

"That's what I said."

"Don't be offended, but why would someone want to buy those?" he asks, trying to figure out which one of the three virtues these items would best fit in. Hope, prosperity, or happiness.

"Why would someone want to buy...seeds

and weeds?" Sarl retorts, leaning over to catch a glimpse of Kip's sign. "I pull weeds and turn them into mulch. And seeds? Are you selling weed seeds? That's dumb. No one wants that."

"At least my product isn't aimed at hurting anyone."

"That's ignorant thinking. I have all sorts of products. These here are colorful fireworks. I got green and purple around here somewhere," he says, holding up some rockets. "...and some of the bigger bags are used for blasting the side off of a mountain or tunneling through a cave mine."

"Do we get a lot of miners in these parts?" Kip asks to further press his point while eye-balling the exploding-tipped arrows that are taking up most of Sarl's table space. Kip knows that there aren't many mountains in the sur-rounding area. Nothing more than a rolling hill exists for miles upon miles.

"What are you getting at?" Sarl looks at Kip curiously.

"Violence only endorses more violence. That is all I am saying."

"You have to fight fire with bigger, hotter fire."

"That logic isn't right," Kip says, shaking his

head back and forth.

"It is my right to protect myself and the people I care about."

"I agree, but by blowing someone up from afar? That isn't simply for protection."

"Look, you don't have to approve of my methods, but that's kind of how explosions work. You don't want to be anywhere near the blast radius when it goes off. Unless of course you want to get blown up too...or hit with some shrapnel."

"I am not against protecting yourself, but why can't people just talk out their problems with the aid of a dagger or a short sword for protection? Anything less drastic."

"Because someone else will have a polearm and stab you before you even get close enough to talk. Look, I didn't make the rules. Ever since arrows and crossbow bolts came on the scene, people are dying before evidence of a threat is known. I am only providing the biggest, deadliest projectile on the market."

"What if it gets in the hands of bad people?"

"It won't."

"How can you be so sure?"

"I look into my customer's eyes, and I can tell what kind of person they are. You can't hide evil, not from me."

"That's it? That's all you do to safeguard your product and the safety of those around you?"

"I am here as a service, not as some morality guard. If some goodly customer leaves their rocket in a place where someone bad can steal it, so be it. Once it leaves my shop, it's out of my hands. I can't be held responsible beyond that." Sarl walks over to a nearby gas-lit lantern and moves it five feet away from his display.

"It is your duty."

"That is an unreasonable request. What do you want me to do, make them sign a promissory note for proper use?"

"I don't have the answers. I just think we need less ways to harm."

"Let me ask you this. Someone buys one of your little seeds and then they take it home and nurture it until it grows into a disastrous spike ball. Then, while making supper, their child stabs out its own eye on one of the weed's spiky bits. Is it your fault for selling them the plant in the first place?"

"No, That is just neglectful parenting."

"Exactly. That's the same thing as my wares. It is just poor bomb etiquette."

"You see, I would still feel responsible for the accident even though it wasn't directly my fault."

"I wouldn't lose any sleep over it because it is out of my control," Sarl admits with a shrug.

"What if someone blew themselves up trying to light one of those firework flares you have?"

"Still not my fault. It isn't my responsibility to follow every customer home to ensure they handle my product with care."

"Don't you care at all?"

"I only care for my own well-being, and making money is how I have to do that."

Puzzled by his crass response, Kip drags his feet back to his table.

Distracted with the potentially life-threatening wares next to him, Kip forgets that his barter vouchers are left on the table unguarded.

Day Two, 6:45 pm: The Incident

Each day of the festival always ends with the artistic parade that slowly makes its way through each of the districts, starting from the arena and ending at the king's courtyard. The theme is a masquerade of happy death. People dress up as smiling ghouls, skeletons and zombies alike.

The message is to show that sometimes in darkness and loss, you can find happiness and levity. The musicians and performance art dancers jaunt through the castle, one street at a time. It is up to the audience to make their very best scary faces as the parade galivants by.

Tonight is loud but highly entertaining. Everyone is welcome to join in, to strut and sing with the extraordinarily dressed concession.

The parade is particularly rowdy due to the multiple events that praise contestants for overindulging on mead. It's all clean fun at the end of the day. Miniature coins are being tossed to everyone participating in exchange for dried black flower petals as a token of luck. "Token for token" is a phase often screamed at voice-cracking levels.

These blessed coins have little to no worth but can be turned in at vendor booths for discounts. Kip has his two small sacks full from avoiding the previous night's escapades. He didn't give out a single coin because he wasn't feeling at all festive. Today, however, proved to be much better on all accounts. Somehow feeling horrible brought in more sales than when he was trying hard to sell. Sometimes you just don't know what people will or will not respond to. It is a game of trial and error. Suffice it to say, Kip is in high spirits and eager to unwind after today's success.

Everyone is equally accepted in the parade—rich or poor, no matter their race or beliefs. All that matters are the quality of the costumes and the amount of fun being had by all.

A feather-dressed woman is beating on a drum while dancing freely past Kip's table. She reminds him of someone, though he knows it is just a colorful costume. It is wonderfully done. He reaches into his sack and tosses a couple handfuls of the novelties, showing his appreciation for her craft.

The woman makes collecting his coins part of her dance choreography, never missing a beat. She blows him a thankful kiss with the air from her lips propelling a single black rose petal towards him.

He snatches it out of the air. Inside his grasp, it feels warm and hopeful, and when he opens his hand, a small bird flies out.

He Looks up in disbelief, though the woman is nowhere to be seen. That was a fun trick, one he couldn't begin to understand.

Feeling uneasy, Kip looks down at his

storage chest. There is a little guilt for having a good time when this trip is supposed to be work, not pleasure.

Rummaging through his stash, he finds that he has fifteen new pits from the day's hard work. Those orbs are the real reason for him being here. He just wants to take a peek to remind himself that he has earned a little bit of relaxation.

After quickly closing the chest, he rests his hand on top of it. "It may have started out slow, but it was a great day."

Looking over at his next-door neighbor, Kip realizes by the scowl on the man's face that this wasn't the right event to be selling explosives, even though it looked promising for him on the first day.

"How did you do?" Kip tries to yell over the good time that is being had by all.

"What do you mean by that?" Sarl asks with a fake smile plastered on his face.

"Nothing, just trying to start a conversation is all."

"Do you want to know how much coin I made?" Sarl asks in protest, his false smile now turning into a real downward frown.

Obviously, Kip had said something to offend

the salesman. "No. I mean, did you gain whatever it was that you wanted by coming here? Like, did you meet some nice people or engage in any good conversations? I come here to buy, not to sell, so monetarily speaking, I lost a bunch of coin but also had a successful day."

"Say it again."

"Excuse me?"

"I want to hear you say it again, what you first said to me."

That is a strange request. Kip suddenly feels like a rabbit caught in the nape by a wolf's mouth without anywhere left to run.

"How did you do? Did you meet any nice people?" Sarl didn't tell him what his purpose for being there was, so he has to guess. But based on Sarl's grumpy attitude, Kip knows without a doubt it was purely for profits.

"Oh, yes, I did," Sarl says, this time with a cheerful tone that wasn't there the first time Kip asked him.

What kind of power move is this? Kip wonders. He meant nothing by his comment but obviously hit a nerve with Sarl. Which tells Kip without a doubt that there is no market for explosives at a fair of happiness and prosperity.

"But no one as nice as me, right?" Kip asks

with a chuckle, trying to make light of the whole awkward moment.

"To be honest, I find you a little annoying, actually," Sarl says with a completely normal smile on his face this time.

That comment takes Kip's breath away, making his heart skip a beat. *How can someone say something so mean while looking so happy saying it?* Either he gets pleasure from Kip's pain, or Sarl is completely two-faced.

For the last two days, Kip has been nothing but overly nice to Sarl, even when faced with his alpha-male antics, like the situation with the table thief. And to think, Kip was going to buy something just to help remedy Sarl's mood.

"Just a little bit?" Kip manages to squeeze out a response, trying to show he isn't completely devastated on the inside, though he actually is.

Sarl tosses Kip a firework. "Hey, didn't you say earlier that you were interested in a rocket?"

Nearly fumbling the explosive, Kip grabs ahold of it with both hands. "Isn't it dangerous?"

Sarl brushes off the danger with a shrug. "That one is five, or three for ten. How many do you want?"

Kip cannot believe that Sarl is still trying to make a sale, what with how he just insulted Kip to his face. There is no way he is going to buy anything from Sarl now. In fact, he has to restrain himself from throwing the explosive as hard as he can right into his smug little face.

A sudden bright green flash scourges through the dark sky like a tentacle. Following the light is a loud explosion that shakes the whole castle. It roughly resembles lightning in a storm.

Kip looks up, but there isn't a cloud in the sky. "Whoa. One of yours?"

"Not mine..."

A moment later, another bright flash slithers through the open end of the castle, and Kip admires its electrically rich colors, though it is almost blindingly bright. This is a new brand of fireworks show.

"A little excessive, wouldn't you agree?" Kip turns to Sarl for answers, but he is gone. "Where did he run off to?"

The mobile party continues, shouting an occasional expression of awe at the skyward lights as they come.

Kip now pays no mind to his missing

neighbor, gingerly placing the firework back on Sarl's table.

Another flash comes, faster than the last.

It is starting to give him a headache, so Kip decides to close his eyes this time. He now starts to see spots in his vision. The aftershock is more violent than the last and knocks over one of Kip's smaller table signs.

Reaching over to try and pick it up, he notices that it has fallen into a puddle of water that's coming from who knows where.

The flashes come more quickly now, each one faster than the last.

Kip is starting to get quite agitated and a little scared. "This is way too much. Can they give it a rest?" Kip says after the next flash, this one much closer than the previous.

Looking down at his fallen sign, from this angle and with the water washing away the paint, what once read "rudimentary specimens" seems to only read "run."

He hears some far-off commotion. Looking around the crowd reveals something strange—people are getting hurt, while the majority of the partygoers are oblivious to it. This is not right. Someone has to warn them.

Day Three, 4:11 am: Demolition

Dust is still stuck in the air from the trampling herd. Kip dodges and weaves around the occasional stray runner that gets in his way. His feet carry him towards the danger this time. He hopes that he isn't too late.

Approaching the place where he was dragged from, he pauses for a moment. A bloody smear mars the ground as a sign of his insolence. "Hog-hugger," he calls himself in anger. "I had no choice. I…" he responds to himself in a higher-pitched voice, as if his personality split into two separate people. A low rumbling growl escapes him.

Heel and toe, Kip walks over to where the elder lady was screaming, knowing what he will most likely find there—another mark of his failure. No matter the outcome, he has to know the truth. But he doesn't find anything there, or any sign of her suffering. Someone must have done what he couldn't; they had to have saved that lady, putting their own well-being aside long enough for decency. He holds back his emotions, trying to be strong—trying to be better.

Time just keeps on going with no resolution in sight. Maybe he can rise to the occasion like whoever helped the lady, or at least he can die trying.

A loud explosion brings a ringing to his ears. It is coming from the direction he was planning on going.

For a moment, Kip sees a flicker of light coming from the highest window of the tower. He wonders if there is a princess up there, like in all those fairytales. Of course, all of these human-built castles are based on those fables. But real life is different. It's cruel and unforgiving, without room for happy endings. Life goes on and on, and eventually we all die in the end.

Kip makes his way through the entrance of the stadium. The hall opens up to a huge, expansive gladiator-style colosseum, with step-seating and three stone pillars with the three flags of virtue blowing in the night's wind.

The inside is dressed and decorated with artistic banners painted by the local youth. Originally, this was the staging place for all the art festivities, but currently there are several small, scattered fires which are burning away their efforts. Everything that isn't on fire has been completely destroyed into colorful rubble.

Kip is regretting not visiting the artist area on the first day when he had the chance. He figured that he had plenty of time for it later. The only problem with later is that it doesn't always come, and this is one of those cases.

Out of nowhere, a rock-spiked projectile smashes into Kip's borrowed helm. A dizziness comes over him as it rattles and spins around.

"Get out of there!" a man shouts, knocking Kip to the ground behind some cover. The ill-fitted helmet falls off his head, the spike lodged inside its steel exterior.

"Why did you do that?" Kip asks the man.

"He's out there, idiot."

"Who is? Wait...Sarl? What are you doing here?" Kip instantly recognizes the man. He has a quiver filled with exploding arrows, but he is without a bow to fire them with.

His vendor mate squints and nods as he realizes who he is yelling at. "Oh...hey. You have to be more careful."

"Are you the one doing this? I knew you had to be up to something with all those explosives. I just never thought you could be so evil." In a fit, Kip tries to scramble out of cover to get away from Sarl.

"Don't be so dense. I am not the problem. I am helping!" Sarl pulls Kip back down to the ground by his boot, protecting him from what lies ahead.

"What do you mean?"

Sarl slowly peeks his head up from their hiding spot before the sounds of rapid bursts continue throughout the arena. "Over there. Don't linger too long or else it might take your head off."

Kip slowly starts to rise.

"Not now, stupid! Wait for the break in the spell."

"Sorry, I didn't know."

"Don't apologize; it's your head, not mine."

"Did you say, 'spell'?"

"This has to be magical in nature. Nothing else would be able to defeat my explosives."

Kip waits as the seemingly endless barrage of energy orbs echoes off everything. He has seen a lot of miraculous things in his life, but never has he considered the possibility that some hocus-pocus magic really existed. Although, this could be a case of Sarl finding mystical reasons as to why his products aren't on the top of the food chain.

Just then the "spell," or whatever it is, stops.

Popping his head out like a ground rodent, Kip scans the destruction to see what Sarl is referring to. Among the shattered carts and trampled pieces of fine art, he finally sees something. It's the giant corpse of a beast with hair, scales, and claws.

Never has Kip seen anything like this. It looks like something out of a legend. Its sharp teeth and long tail give Kip a reality adjustment. *First magic, and now dragons?*

After a second glance, he realizes it's not the mythical creature he thought it was at first. He finds the error in his ways after noticing its armored exoskeleton, which is cracked and leaking white liquid. It is almost like a furry crab mixed with a wolf.

This is much worse than any dragon or griffin, because those things are creatures of the imagination. This creature is very much real and seems to be capable of far worse than any myth that Kip has heard.

"What is it?"

"Not sure. All I know is that once it died, the sky stopped lighting up."

"Did you...slay it?" Kip asks.

"No, those other people claimed that thing an hour or so ago." Sarl points an arrow over to the far end of the arena. "I was the one that invited them to the party."

Kip takes another peek, this time waiting for

the break in the continuous popping sound, and sure enough, there is a huge pile of broken stones and other rubble in the stands. Sarl must have been responsible for both letting the adventurers in and releasing the trampling herd of people out. *He is a hero—a rude, self-righteous, honest-to-goodness hero.*

"Where are they now?" Kip asks, but Sarl has already left his side during the break in the firepower. Noticing all the corpses lying next to the felled beast, Kip has a partial answer to his question...dead.

Kip scrambles to catch up to his neighbor who is now fifty feet away.

The rapid attacks start again, each flash lighting up the arena like a strobe. Kip feels as if he is moving in stop motion; each step is staggered. The light orbs that fly by destroy everything in their path.

"What are you doing?" Sarl yells at Kip, but he is too disoriented to think straight, let alone find his way back to cover.

Sarl sprints over to Kip and tackles him to the ground for a second time.

"Ouch, get off me," Kip protests, feeling mild discomfort from where he landed and the heaviness of Sarl's larger frame on top of him.

Only now Sarl isn't responding.

Wondering if he's waiting for another break in the attack, Kip tries to calm his nerves. *He is helping me, not trying to cause me harm. In a moment, we can get out of here. Everything will be okay.*

Finally there is a break in the onslaught in what feels like forever. This gives him the opportunity to move again. He pulls himself out from under Sarl and makes his way back whence he came. He notices that Sarl is not moving.

Kip turns back to collect him and sees three smoking holes radiating from Sarl's back. He was hit by some light orbs while trying to save Kip. It is his fault. Everything is.

Grabbing him by the hand, Kip pulls, but he won't budge.

Faster than before, the light ball attack starts back up again. This time he notices it coming out of the tower.

Aided by adrenaline, Kip tries again, and suddenly he is successful in moving the much heavier fellow. With light orbs at his back, Kip pulls Sarl through the wreckage. He closes his eyes so as to not get disoriented again.

They are safe, taking refuge behind the

fallen beast. The last of the attacks splat into the monstrous body between them and the tower.

"Sarl, Sarl! Can you hear me?" Kip rolls over the lifeless body but gets no response. "Please wake up. I got you out of there."

But Sarl still doesn't respond.

As long as that magic thing is out there, nowhere is safe to hide. Kip feels horrible about the animosity he felt towards the man.

"Why did you save me? I thought you hated me," Kip wants to stay mad at Sarl for his insults, for him making Kip feel like less than nothing, but it was more than that. People can be rude and mean one minute, but heroic and kind the next. Some people are just destined to succeed, and others...are just normal.

Sarl saved Kip. He didn't have to, but he did. This is how Kip learns that life isn't simply black or white. Sometimes bad people are capable of good things, and the opposite is also just as true.

After a long-fought battle, Kip knows that Sarl has found the only peace he was ever going to find—the afterlife.

To Break a Will

"Compassion is a trait mostly embodied by the poor—those who have nothing are willing to give it away. Wealth and greed are a marriage built on the pain and suffering of others. When you have a lot to lose, you hold on to it with both hands while sinking to the bottom of the lake. What treasure is worth dying for? Is anything really more valuable than time? In hindsight, the answer is very simple, though it wasn't always so cut and dry, not from my perspective, anyhow.

"I liked my things - loved them, in fact—maybe a little more than I actually liked myself. People measure you by your things and judge you accordingly. I traveled many miles to accumulate my lifestyle. I might not be a good person, but I have a great deal of things to prove my relevance. I had to exchange time, relationships, and family to acquire it all. Someone changes the rules, and in an instant it all goes up in smoke. Ideas are so fragile. Strangers must have thought me to be quite happy. Here I thought I was, even though I had no one to share my prizes with. The greatest things cannot be held, envied, or gawked at. They rest behind your eyes. And as I slip away, I'm already starting to forget what they are..." *-Benny the Merchant, age unfathomable.*

Day Two, 7:40 pm: The Kindness of Strangers

In the cover of the night, pockets of people have formed group hiding places, sacrificing comfort for the good of the many.

Kip has gotten to know many in this spot and is acting as a runner, or a scout, guiding the misguided to safety. In the middle of this selfless act, he spots the wealthy man who tried to rough him up earlier screaming at a vendor who sells flying suits. The shop is undoubtably closed at the moment. There is a war going on—

of course they're closed.

The vendor desperately tries to flee, but the wealthy man won't let him go until he accepts the piles of coin vouchers he keeps shoving into the vendor's coat pockets.

Noticing this behavior, Kip decides to step in once again.

"Take it. I have more than you'll ever know what to do with," the wealthy man says.

Kip never had a good thought about bullies, and today is no different. "Dead men don't need vouchers, you self-righteous fool," Kip says softly to himself. Heavy-footed, he makes his way over to the confrontation, ignoring the disaster erupting from everywhere.

"Take whatever you want. I don't care. Just let me find my loved ones," the vendor pleads.

"I told you already, not until you show me how to use it!" the wealthy man protests.

"Take your hands off of him!" Kip says, reaching the flying suit booth, which has already been ransacked by looters.

"It has to be you." The wealthy man rolls his eyes upon seeing Kip.

Kip's sore neck also remembers the wealthy man from a little while ago.

"You can't just treat people this way."

"Now you listen to me for a change. Don't you have anything better to do than keep trying to ruin my life?" the wealthy man interrupts, pointing a finger at Kip.

"No. I mean, yes. I do have better things to do. But, no, I am not trying to ruin your life. I am trying to save it."

"You could've fooled me."

The distraction of their argument gives the vendor enough time to get out of the wealthy man's grasp and slip away into the chaos of the crowds.

"Are you happy now? He got away. You doomed us both."

"Yes, I am happy. You were robbing that poor man."

"I was going to buy you a lesson too, but you had to ruin it for the both of us."

"No, you were not. That's a complete fabrication of the truth. Don't try and change the past to make yourself look good."

"Fabrication of the truth? You mean lie?"

"Yes. That too!"

"You're such a miserable human being. You know that, right?"

Shocked by the wealthy man's assumption, Kip loses his words. "I...I..."

The wealthy man picks up two flying suits and looks back and forth for the lost vendor.

It is people like him that make it harder to save the more deserving people. Kip has to not let this man get to him, not again. "Why do you need two suits?" Kip asks, finally finding his voice again.

"Because I want them."

"Just leave one for someone else to find it. Maybe they can get out of this place."

"Oh, you mean leave it for you. No thank you. Knowing my luck, you will crash into me right before reaching safety."

"I wasn't talking about me!"

The man ignores Kip and walks away casually, paying him no importance.

Letting out a deep sigh, Kip wonders how many times he is going to let this wealthy jerk get the best of him. The truth, he knows, is far too depressing to voice out loud. Instead, a lie will have to do, "Never again."

Day Four, 2:58 pm: Bridging the Gap

Avoiding his own shadow, Kip carries on through the open courtyard moving towards the new threat that is terrorizing everybody in sight. *Whatever it is, it attacks differently now. Is it getting weaker or stronger?*

He has no clue how many lives have been lost, or even how many will not last the next nightfall. It has all become a haze in the back of his mind. All he knows is he can't do anything in the form of fighting that will harm or defeat this god-like threat. No one can. He isn't the only one to come to this conclusion either.

Things are awfully quiet around here. His purpose is only to try to help before there is nothing left to save—nothing left of himself. Now he has some fight left in him someone to protect. Almost like a miracle, he has found his bravery.

The tearing, almost ripping sound is getting louder with every step he takes forward. Even still, his steps are pure and sure-footed. Torn streamers and brightly colored decorations blow in the opposite direction, almost as a warning to head the other way fast and without looking back. Kip ignores them and forces himself into the belly of the beast.

The eastern section of the castle is completely in ruins. Smoke billows to the sky as a sign of surrender. A yellow hue fills the air, giving an apocalyptic glow. From an artistic perspective, is it is quite beautiful in a devastating, end-of-days sort of way.

Kip has to move forward, not because he is the smartest, fastest or most qualified. He continues on because he is the only one left willing to try. Or so he thinks, based on the empty streets he has been walking along for quite some time now.

This castle took close to a century to construct. Nearly every boulder was quarried from a 100-miles radius and transported here on the backs of slaves and hired hands. Yet, in less than two days it has been almost completely reduced to rubble. This is the kind of power they're dealing with—something that has a comparable magnitude to a dragon, although there is no such thing as the fictional beast here, outside of story books.

Knowing the full extent of the peril he is up against, he continues forward.

Tired of failure, tired of waiting for someone else to pave his path for him, tired of helping those who choose to give up—mentally, physically, emotionally he has had enough, and enough is enough until there is nothing left.

Judging by the path of destruction, he is on

the right path. Its weakness is that it can only be in one place at a time. There are far too many people to kill swiftly.

A loud rat-a-tat-tat sound is coming from the temple ahead. It can only be described as quick consecutive bursts of sharp explosions. Light flickers through the stained-glass windows from the inside. The resistance must be in there, maybe far less than he thought previously—maybe only three.

Upon pinpointing its location, Kip rushes towards the danger head-on.

The attack is relentless, with a flash, flash, flash...flash, flash, flash...

He knows that each flicker of light is another life ending. It just won't stop. He can't move his legs fast enough.

This evil knows no boundaries. It takes everything, leaving nothing left but annihilation in its path of mayhem. Children, the elderly, the helpless, and beggars—there is no one exempt from the death that it brings.

Flash, flash, flash...

"This has gone on way too long." Without a weapon or a plan or anything at all to aid him in defeating this unmatched power, he runs with the one thing he has left...himself.

Flash, flash, flash...

He has seen many men and woman much better than him, seasoned fighters, trained warriors, explosion experts, and they all had the same conclusion—death. It's now Kip's turn, and all he can ask for is dying with his head held tall, not in the ground like an ostrich.

Flash, flash, flash, flash...

Kip runs right through the front room of the temple, sliding on the broken glass and shattered wood as he comes to an awkward stop.

The temple is silent. Holy pages are floating down to the ground like the endless leaves of fall. There are no more men of the cloth around. They have long since abandoned the whole thing.

Corpses are lying over pews and scattered everywhere. There are a few parishioners on their knees, praying for salvation, thinking their gods and goddesses will protect them inside the sanctuary.

There is only one higher power present inside this holiest of places, and it isn't in the business of saving anyone or anything.

Kip recognizes the madman straightaway. Wearing a golden robe that is now charred with burnt blood, it is the cause of everything—the sole being that is doing all this harm. It is the one and only Mad Wizard. He is just one person, a man, not a band of assassins or a war party, like previously speculated. Not some beautiful angel or other mythical creature sent here to invoke judgment. It is just a scrawny-looking person with dry skin. A person. That is the craziest of concepts for Kip to come to terms with. How can one person do such a heinous act? It doesn't make any sense.

"Over here, you piece of shit," Kip screams at the wizard who is firing short blasts out of his hands at helpless temple-goers. Never has Kip used such language in his life. But in the moment, the ire, or maybe the spirit of the False Knight is with him, and it feels right.

Flash, flash... the wizard turns to Kip with a bright glowing fist, enchanted dark eyes, and bearing wicked gnarled teeth...

Day Three, 1:05 am: Giving the Goat

The battle seems to be going on forever, even though it has only been throughout the night. Exhaustion and hunger fill the ranks of exhausted warriors as they fight with everything they have against the unspeakable power.

Catching everyone's attention is a person

yelling sharp sounds of jubilation. "See you later, fools!"

Kip wonders where such a seemingly happy statement is coming from in such a ravaged battleground as this. Looking up, he soon has his question answered.

Overhead, there is a person in a flight suit soaring through the night's sky like a bat. He is undoubtably the culprit.

Having climbed up some rafters to help a trapped goat, Kip ducks just in time to avoid getting a new haircut by the man buzzing by.

"It just had to be you!" the man in the suit yells at Kip.

That voice? It takes him a beat, but Kip soon realizes that it's the wealthy man from before who is fleeing the battle like the man said he would—with the stolen flying suit.

For a moment, Kip imagines himself flying next to the guy. Even though that was never an actual possibility, he can almost feel the freeing sensation of the wind underneath his stolen wings. A pang of jealousy comes over him.

Why do jerks always manage to bully their way ahead of everyone else? Kip shakes his head back and forth at the sight.

Earlier in the festival, Kip unintentionally

cut a line for cart service and ended up having to hand-carry his stuff as a result. He always gets in trouble or punished for such bold acts, whether intentional or not. Other people have all the luck and get away with practically murder. As much as he would love to escape this living hellscape, never would he choose to trade his dignity for a seat next to that despicable excuse for a human being.

Kip doesn't want to let him get away that easily. He looks down at his rope—thoughts of lassoing the flying man and tying him up like a hog bring a smile to Kip's dirt-covered face. "Just let him go. He isn't worth the effort." The man's money and privilege may have bought him a way out of this nightmare, but he has to live with himself, and that is a fate worse than death.

Taking the high road, like always, Kip salutes the man from the top of his armored helm, sincerely wishing him a safe journey.

The man laughs hysterically at Kip's effort. "This could have been you. It could have been."

Yes, perhaps he is right, but then that would also mean that Kip wouldn't have been himself. No one with a shred of decency could just fly away—not if they ever wanted to sleep soundly ever again. If that's the price of freedom, the cost is far too rich for Kip...or any person of character.

Just then, the wealthy man crashes head-first into a tower wall and tumbles to the ground, end over end like a stone rolling down a hill.

Kip can't help but cringe at the crunching noise the man makes when he hits the ground.

The wealthy man isn't moving or insulting anyone else, not ever again. He really should have taken a helmet before taking flight in the strange contraption. That or a simple helmet.

A myriad of emotions come at him all at once; guilt, sorrow, fear, anger, and jealousy, to name a few. With envy filling his eyes, Kip thinks about how that is the real exit his patience is fighting with. He could never live with himself if he fled the good fight. But...what if he didn't have to? What if the end found him first? He starts to feel as though his body is lighter than ever before.

"I bet I could also fly, if I really wanted to," Kip says in a monotone way. His eyes are fixated on the ground below. Slowly he lets his grip on the rafter go limp. "The nothingness is calling to me."

The goat bleats out a toothy sound as a taunt. The sound snaps Kip out of his destructive thoughts. There is no time for such things, not when a goat needs to be got.

Crawling on the rafters on all fours, Kip has a better vantage point to watch the battle brewing off in the distance. He marvels at the fitness and aptitude of the warriors' combined efforts.

The heavily armored warriors are taking the brunt of the physical attacks coming from a far-off tower. Archers shoot metal rods in the air to redirect the electric assaults—following the lead of the False Knight.

Slow and steady, the brave band inch their way closer to the tower inside the far end of the arena. *Of course, the high ground.* This is where the foes have all the advantage.

Although the adventuring party has no way of getting into the inner sanctum, still they move forward, trading casualties with every advance they make.

Whatever lies in the tower is much stronger than anything Kip has ever seen, or even fathomed seeing.

These are the finest warriors of these parts, and they are melting away faster than snow in the desert. Yet they fight and push on, never breaking for food, to catch their breath or even to go to the bathroom.

Kip watches a fighter leading the charge, fall after getting hit by a black orb that takes half of his face along with it.

Another warrior is quick to upgrade his own shield with that of the fallen compatriot, now serving as the new leading party member.

The biggest of the lot is the man who gave Kip the helm. He has two armored corpses over each of his shoulders, using them as protection. He is by far the strongest, almost giant-like. Still he struggles against the force coming from the tower. Different colors and attacks rain down upon them in staggering numbers. It almost looks beautiful from this lookout, like moon bugs lighting up the sky during a summer solstice.

Fixating on the goat, Kip scales the thin plank. Slowly he moves in a little closer, trying to ignore the destruction below, above, and all around. Saving animals is more his speed.

Just as he gets within arm's reach, the goat leaps up on a nearby pole that used to hold an oil street lamp.

"Come on, buddy. Don't do this to me," Kip pleads with the old kid, but he isn't giving up that easily.

Like a squat frog, Kip leaps out of the air and snatches the goat off the pole. Together they're heading straight for the hard stone ground below.

Tucking into a ball around the goat, Kip takes the brunt of the impact directly on his shoulder and rolls over himself a couple times.

Wheezing and gasping, Kip cannot get air to his lungs. He must have knocked the wind out of himself from the fall. Instincts want him to panic, but he knows better. *It will pass; just give it time.*

While Kip is distracted, the goat manages to free itself from his huddled grasp—unharmed from the interaction.

This could be it—drowning in a waterless grave. He decides not to fight it and let the time pass by naturally.

Is this really my time? If so, I wonder what they would put on my tombstone if I were to ever have one. "Kip—he got that goat."

Then, like a tidal wave of air, he regains his breath and inhales deeply. He takes it all into his sore lungs. After a couple giant heaving breaths like this, his breathing becomes steady once again. He rises to his feet and looks around, wondering if anyone witnessed his mighty rescue.

No one saw. *Oh, well.*

Rotating his shoulder lets out a couple of loud ticks and clicks, but he doesn't feel a thing. He must have fallen on it just right, or just right enough.

It is somehow easier for him to save a goat than humans. Goats don't judge you. Or if they do, it's in a language he will never understand. Plus, he never would have tried a stunt like that with a child, fearing that he might hurt or kill it by accident. But with the goat, the thought didn't even cross his mind.

Using his rope, Kip makes a loop and drags the goat back to the triage area. Right away, a nurse rushes over to him with two babies bundled up in her arms. "You did it! How did you manage?"

Kip looks down at the two hungry babes and smiles widely. "It wasn't easy, but it was well worth the effort."

A couple helpers take off the rope and instantly start to milk the animal. One of the helpers tosses Kip back his rope.

"I was planning on letting you keep it, but okay." Kip puts it back into his bag.

"Thank you so much. You're a real hero to these two."

"It's what anyone would do." Kip is feeling on top of the world. The nurse said the one thing he always wanted to hear, and he saw clearly in her eyes that she meant it.

A sudden surge of bravery comes over him. He holds on tightly to his loose-fitting helm and makes a break for it. He runs out of the triage area, through the first battlefield, down the dark alley, through the retaining wall for respite, down some winding steps and back down to the front lines—glowing projectiles flying past his ears as he runs.

Cheers and chants erupt from the wounded and dying. He doesn't know why or how, but he is going with everything he has. He doesn't know what he will do once he gets there, yet he pushes onward.

Rushing into the battlefront, he hears, "Go get 'em, kid!" from the strongest bearded warrior, now showing him the respect he withheld when he gave Kip the helm.

Things graze across the surface of Kip's flesh and rip through his clothes, though they are luckily just scrapes, and his adrenaline is protecting him from a certain level of pain—if not all of it. So far, nothing hurts enough to stop his surefooted sprint, so he keeps going. He's the leader now, rushing past everyone.

Dead ahead, Kip makes his way up the grand steps straight towards the focal point of the whole castle—the king's quarters.

A Crushing Disposition

"Nothing is real, nor was it ever. People hide behind false grins and unintentional promises without follow-through or being held accountable for any of it. Emotions, however, are very much real. They affect us in disguise and infest deep inside our subconscious, molding our personalities like a sculptor. Fake actions produce real emotions that wound or repair a soul. Choose your interactions wisely, because it could very well end you. I've put a lot of dangerous things inside my mouth but nothing as dangerous as the words I say now.

"One by one, the killing continued without a word as to why, never stopping or slowing. It knew only one thing, death, and it brought it in quickly and in abundance. Days went by without any change. It was coming for us all, one at a time.

"The lucky ones met a quick end, never knowing the tortures that the less fortunate had to endure. I rushed into the torrent to save an elder. Without warning, I became a stepping-stone for others to reach salvation. No matter how much pain I felt or how loud I cried, I was nothing more than a means to an end. But little did they know it would be their time soon enough." -*Salvo the Firebreather, age 21.*

Day Four, 3:41 pm: Not on My Watch

People are wounded, dead, and in some cases halfway in between.

What is he thinking standing up to a power as great as this? Time seems to be at a standstill for the moment. Slowly he feels his lungs fill with air. He has figured out the mystery that has been plaguing him for so long, yet it is all too late.

This is my last breath. I better savor it.

He knows that there won't be any time for him to exhale. This thing kills fast.

Some foreign object shatters through a stain

glass window and inches its way across the room with purpose. It looks like a series of hooks on a rope, or something similar.

Following the slowness of time, the wizard turns its attack towards the object, but it's too late.

The diversion Kip made has served as a good enough distraction to allow the hooks to clamp down like a mouth onto the wizard's form, pulling him through the hole it came out of.

Instantly, when the wizard leaves the vicinity, time returns to normal.

Falling to his knees, Kip's heart is pounding hard and fast. *This was a horrible idea. Maybe my worst yet.*

Changing tactics, Kip tries to blend in, abandoning any acts of heroism. His goal is to become an object rather than a target. This is all in order to be overlooked in the chaos of the day. He slows his breathing, keeping his movements almost unnoticeable. Closing his eyes would be a dead giveaway to his very much alive state. Instead, he opts to give off a blank stare. His eyes are fixated on a broken candelabra, as opposed to one of the many bodies scattered on the ground, toppled over furniture, or slumped against the wall. It is the only place in his line of sight that isn't featuring the dead and dismembered.

Thinking of one of the saddest faces Kip had to say goodbye to, a thick wave of despondence comes over him. She smelled nice and begged him to stay, but he couldn't just sit there and hide, not when he had something to live for, a life to protect. Now he is doing the exact thing he tried so hard to avoid. His sad eyes are the perfect disguise for his feigned death, that is, if he doesn't begin to cry.

Everything is set. All he has to do now is wait it out. That is what everyone else is doing anyway. He already tried to be a hero and tried to run; now it is time for something new.

Someone or something is stirring, and that means he isn't alone.

Holding his breath, Kip tries to think of nothing, to become nothing.

Step by step, the someone is getting closer. Inch by inch, they close the gap from the doorway to where Kip is playing possum.

One false move and that *thing* can vaporize him in an instant—just like it did to so many before him. If everyone is slain, there will be no one left to tell the story. Kip is determined to be that person.

Back at the bridge, some people did manage to escape, but they left long before things really started to get ugly. Who knows if they just ran to get help or simply just ran. Kip has to keep hope alive. He has to believe they all didn't just selfishly run for cover, though he wouldn't blame them if they did. Something has to come and put an end to all this suffering.

Whatever is stirring is nearly upon him now and must have seen right through his façade.

Should I run or be patient? What other choices do I have?

Following some rustling of papers, Kip's eyes shift to see the silhouette of a figure dancing across the stone walls and broken stain-glass window.

The more he tries to keep his gaze fixed, hallow, and vacant, the more his eyes dart directly at the source of all the ruckus, exposing his dead giveaway. Lucky for him, it isn't in fact a killer. Rather, it's a grave robber. Only these graves are not yet dug.

Kip takes in a deep breath and lets out a quiet sigh of relief.

One after another, the thief slides rings off of cold fingers, breaks the clasps of necklaces from around tortured faces, lifts ornate weapons, belts, and anything else that isn't stained by too much blood and gore. The figure loots without prejudice or consideration for whom he is taking from. He only takes a brief moment to inspect the authenticity of an item by banging or biting on it.

It is despicable, completely nasty, and undoubtedly quite profitable. The thief already has two large bags and a medium pouch nearly bursting at the seams with treasure. At this rate, he will need a cart to pull all of his goods.

Never having had interest in coins or the greed that comes with them, Kip wonders what kind of scum would use a situation like this to seek to profit off the downfall of others. On the other hand, the thief is brave enough to be walking around with that *thing* out there. That's more than what Kip is doing, and that has to count for something. But does one act of bravery justify such an act of greed?

One lady suddenly has a burst of energy and is holding on to her bracelet, not letting it out of her grasp.

Not only is Kip surprised to find someone else doing the same thing as him, playing dead, but she isn't going to give up her belongings without a fight. He would give the tunic off his back fast and easy so that he can get back to his motionless silence. But no, she's holding on to it as if she were holding on to dear life.

Back and forth, they argue at each other with a series of grunts, neither of them letting go.

How far will this guy's greed take him, Kip wonders. The thief is determined to take this particular bracelet, even though his whole arm is filled with similar bangles and bands. What is so great about this woman's artifact? It's not like there is a lack of other items for him to take without asking. At this rate, he's going to get them all killed.

As things escalate, the thief strikes the woman with a closed fist wrapped in jewels. It only takes a couple of hits until she gives up on the fight. It's one of those days where you've been pushed way past your limit and would literally die over a silly little bracelet.

This is not right. She is defenseless on the ground, and the thief still starts to rummage through her pockets for more.

Kip can't just sit here and watch this happen, can he? *What would I do if I actually had the courage to do anything about it?* While debating with himself about fear and heroics, he is already on his feet and tapping the thief on his hunched- over back.

It appears that Kip's body doesn't want to wait for his mind to decide to take action. "Excuse me?" Kip greets the thief with a gruff look about him.

As the thief turns around, his face is met with Kip's open-handed slap, knocking him to the ground. Jewels and coins scatter everywhere.

It wasn't a pretty or particularly clean hit, but the tip of Kip's finger did manage to jab inside the thief's eye.

"Are you crazy?" the thief hisses, rubbing his tearing eye with his forearm.

The elderly lady flashes Kip an encouraging nod, raising her fist high in the air.

With a crazed look in his eyes, Kip stares the thief down with a "come try me" face.

They size each other up, waiting to see who makes the next move.

"Give it back," Kip says in a low—well, low for him—yet serious voice.

The thief leans his head back while hocking up some spit to...

That's it. Without hesitation, Kip's booted

foot catches the thief's throat, making him choke on the projectile he was producing.

"I said give it back! This has been a particularly bad day for me, and by the looks of it, her too. You, however, don't give a damn about anything or anyone. I am guessing this is one of the best days of your filthy, pathetic, rotten life." Kip twists his foot back and forth to really rub in his point.

"People like you are what is exactly wrong with the realm. You ruin everything for people like me who only want to follow the stupid rules. Well, not anymore. You give this nice lady back her charm right now. It is the only thing she has left to hold on to in this world and stopping you is the only thing I have. She is willing to die over it, I am willing to kill over it, The only question is, are you willing to let go of it?"

The thief wastes no time in throwing the bracelet back to the woman—well, more like near her—but that is good enough for Kip.

Kip releases his foot, the thief instantly throws up all over himself and his bag of goodies while clamoring for breath.

His hacking and wheezing echo throughout the temple. This is becoming a scene—a loud spectacle.

The silence of the outside turns into an ever-growing sizzle. This is not good. The thing outside heard them; their altercation was too loud.

Feeling big quickly fades, because now the very thing Kip was hiding from might be coming straight for him.

Day Three, 4:27 am: Over His Head

Taking cover behind an enormous dead beast in the arena, sits Kip. Right next to the man who gave his life for his. *Why couldn't I have saved his life instead?*

Kip knew the answer to his own question before he asked it of himself. Life isn't about equality or just and fair endings. Nor is it part of some grand scheme or even something more intimate. Life is mayhem, and this is it at its worst.

This is the end of happiness, the end of innocence, and possibly the end of existence. How can anything go up against such powerful foes and win?

Hot smoke disappears into the sky from the wounds on Sarl's back like steam from a freshly poured cup of tea.

After the guilt of Kip's actions sink in, his teeth won't stop chattering, matching his hand's movements. "I'm sorry...so s...sorry." But no words can bring him back. This has not been a good day for existence.

"I'm not done for," Sarl says groggily and gruffly.

"What?" tears of happiness fill Kip's eyes as

he sets them upon whom he thought he had lost forever.

"Not yet, anyway."

"Are you okay? I mean...are you hurt?"

"Don't ask stupid questions. I have holes in me."

"I...didn't mean to."

"Look, I need you to do something for me. There isn't a lot of time, so listen carefully." Sarl struggles to move his limp body. "Take this detonator and finish what I've started."

Reaching out into the open, Kip quickly pulls his hand back as if touching something sharp. "I can't. I'm too afraid."

"It's too late for me. You must be my will."

"I am no hero. I am a coward."

No longer able to hold up his head, Sarl flops down nearly defeated. "I know you are... but cowards can do great things too. Come on, take this," Sarl says, reaching out his balled-up fist to Kip. "It will help."

"What...what is it?" Kip gently places his hand under Sarl's, thinking it is the detonator he spoke of.

Sarl opens his hand to reveal that nothing is there. "I give you my courage. You can borrow it until I need it again," Sarl says.

"I don't understand."

"You don't have to understand. Just take it!" Sarl places his hand inside Kip's. Their warmth meets through the touch.

Even though courage and fear can't be traded or interchanged like some kind of commodity, it somehow makes Kip feel better in a strange sort of way.

"What do I do with it?"

Sarl gently taps the metal rod that's resting near his feet. "Take this to my beautiful arrangement over there." Sarl tries to point, but he doesn't have the energy left in him.

Feeling energized, Kip slides on his stomach, snatching the long stick without giving any pause.

In one fluid motion, he leaps to his feet and continues out into the open arena.

Stone projectiles whiz past his head and crash into something behind him while he makes the maneuver.

The false courage keeps him safe throughout the journey towards shelter behind a fallen statue. What remains of the crumbled face looks at him almost encouragingly. Like all art, you see what you want or need to, not what the artist had intended.

Sarl coughs up a spot of blood as he tries to speak.

Time is making Kip regress back to himself, with more of Sarl's blood on his hands—especially now that he is literally seeing it. "Oh, no!" Kip's confidence dips slightly.

"Don't worry about me. Take...all my courage, every last drop...and light...it...up." Sarl's finger indicates the location of a wick to his trap off in the distance.

"But..."

"Go...hurry."

Without wasting any more precious time, Kip does as he is instructed. Pushing all of his fears down to his legs, he moves like he never has before—quick and agile like a sickle cat. Magical attacks come at him from all directions. The bad men must be surrounding him, as he gives it everything he's got.

Reaching down, he drags the detonating rod against the cobble-stone ground. It instantly sparks, leaving a trail of flashing light behind him. He only has one crack at this, and he wants to make sure the detonator is extremely hot and ready for the task.

Running in an arch, he feels like the rain god creating a rainbow of prismatic sparks against the stone ground. It doesn't take long for the tip of the metal rod to ignite into a multi-colored flare.

He's on track to reach the fuse before the fire dies down.

Without looking back, Kip heaves the flaming rod at the pile of fuses, which are neatly and thoughtfully tied together near the base of the king's tower. Coated in a flammable compound, the wicks twinkle as they burn towards their intended destinations. It is a spiderweb made up of fiery paths that run towards their respective destinations.

One at a time, explosions go off in all directions, rupturing the whole area in a deep rumble.

A thick shockwave knocks Kip off his feet. That is the biggest of the series of explosions.

In succession, bright colorful lights launch into the air, making it appear to be a great celebration. And if this works, it will be.

As the walls fall and crumble into the arena, so does the large tower at the end of the structure. This is the true intention of Sarl's trap, to level the playing field—no longer giving whatever was in the tower the highest of grounds.

As the heavy stone and debris tumble on top

of each other, Kip catches a glimpse of a figure inside the King's tower just before dust and dirt cover everything.

He isn't exactly sure who was inside there, but one thing is for sure, it wasn't a king.

Once the show is over, all that remains of the tower is a huge pile of rocks. No one could have survived such a devastating avalanche of stone.

The attacks have stopped with the fall of the tower. Sarl had a truly supreme plan, one that seemed to put things back to rest.

Kip crawls to his feet, pumping a fist into the air. He did it, and he survived to tell the tale.

Turning his gratitude to his neighbor, Kip's courage and excitement instantly dissipates into the heavens when he notices that his hero really has passed away this time.

"We did it," Kip says a little more humbled, trying to show his respects.

Never has Kip seen someone die with such a joyous smile on their face. It is haunting, yet beautiful. Sarl died for something, and Kip is living proof of his glory. His only hope is that Sarl managed to see his destruction in action before he passed. Judging by his expression, he had to have seen its splendor—everyone did.

"What is that?" Kip turns suddenly upon hearing the grinding sound of rock on rock.

"There it is again," he says, turning to the fallen tower, realizing where the sound is coming from. This isn't just the sound of the earth settling. Something is moving or—more importantly—someone.

The truth is hard to swallow, but truth it is. Whatever was in the tower is still alive, and Kip alone is about to face it.

Kip takes one step forward, his good nature pushing him to give a helpful hand, though he second-guesses himself instantly.

No. Whatever is trapped in there is an entity of pure evil.

No normal being could have survived such a fall. That must mean...

Rock and stone rubble start to roll off the mound without any indication as to how or why.

Kip takes in a huge breath and stands there dumbfounded as the rocks and rubble dislodge themselves from the wreckage as if they have a mind of their own.

Terrified, Kip shakes and shivers uncontrollably, awaiting what is to come next.

Out of the tower ruins, a golden-robed

figure emerges, seemingly unscathed from the avalanche of stones.

This god-like figure looks directly at Kip with bright prismatic eyes. Kip feels as if his consciousness is being sucked into his round orbs. It is as if he is peering into an endless sea of souls, more plentiful than the stars above. Instead of waves, they are silent screams from the dead mouthing warnings of retreat.

Run. Come on, legs, just move. No matter what Kip tries to do, his body is unresponsive. He feels a warm liquid running down his leg, as if things couldn't get any worse.

The dark one ominously reaches his hand up and points it directly at Kip. Starting from his fingertips, his hand starts to glow brightly through a round object inside his clutched hand.

That object...it looks familiar to him, almost as if it's calling to him, but he is too scared and in the moment to try to search his memory to place it.

This is it, the end of him, dying a disgraceful death in a puddle of his own urine.

Day Four, ███████: I Have to Go

Inside the perfectly black sewers, Kip and the widow are taking very a lovely stroll. Not being able to see makes Kip feel as though he can be whoever he wants.

"What's your name? I don't know if I forgot it or if you never told me. Sorry. I am very embarrassed to even ask," Kip says wanting to know where to place his feelings for her.

"Names are nothing special. No matter how unique you think yours is, someone else somewhere always shares it with you."

"Don't you want me to know your name?"

"Why is it so important?"

"What if I want to write you a letter? To whom do I address it?" Kip says, stopping to turn to her in the darkness. Not that he is prone to writing letters, but it is the only example he can come up with on the spot. "Don't you want to know my name?"

"I don't need to know your name; I already know what to call you," she says with a coy undertone.

"And what might that be?"

Even though he cannot see her expression, he can almost feel her smile as bright as a beacon of light. After a beat, Kip knows that she isn't going to tell him, not yet anyhow.

They continue walking, a little bit closer to each other than before.

After a while, they pass by a pocket of putrid-smelling stuff. They cuddle in close together taking in each other's scent instead of the alternative. She smells flowery and soft despite everything she must have gone through to get to this point.

"You smell like a hero," the woman says softly.

"I don't think so, but thank you anyway."

"No, you do," she reiterates, taking in a deeper breath this time.

"How does a hero even smell? Sweaty? Hard working?"

"No. Safe...like home."

Kip's happy that she cannot see the redness that is coming over his face. That is by far the sweetest thing anyone has ever said to him. What makes it even more touching is that she didn't have to say it. But she did, and he has a silly suspicion that she actually meant it.

***

They reach the end of the line. Without a torch

or other light source, it seems that they might be walking around in circles. Even though they enjoyed the conversation and each other's company, without food or any potable water, their energy is wearing thin.

"Let's stop for a while," Kip says, finding a quiet corner. Using just his sense of touch, he lays the woman down in a dry spot in the dead end. Slowly he tucks her in with the blanket he has.

"I think you will be safe here."

"You mean we will, right?"

"Well...I suppose..."

"No, don't leave me in the darkness," she says, sensing his desperation. "Everyone leaves me. First my family, then my late husband. I can't handle being alone."

"I would come back."

"Don't you want to stay?"

Kip curls up next to her, sharing his warmth. "Of course I do." Using his free hand, Kip strokes her hair gently, slowly removing the dead flowers that used to be part of her wedding attire.

"I am happy," she said softly.

Let the world crumble and burn all around him; he can't leave her.

He continues petting her until they both fall fast asleep.

***

Abruptly Kip wakes from his unexpected slumber. There is no way of judging how many minutes or hours have passed. He doesn't dare move and chance waking her. Torn, Kip knows that he has abandoned all the duties topside to stay with her. Except this is the strongest connection he has ever felt to someone else.

She is confused; her husband just died. How can I know for sure what is real and what is just her being lonely?

This is the most inopportune time to start a great romance. He hates that he had to find her in the worst day of his life, because now it is also the best.

He stays awake for many more hours watching over her. It is hard enough to discern what day it is, let alone the hour. After a spell, diffused light starts to pour in through a grate overhead. The morning dew makes her almost shimmer. She is much more stunning than he remembers.

Only with the break of day upon them does

something catch his eye. The fur-lined fabric she is sleeping on, it has a tag on it. He knows that logo well. It is one made by his vendor friend Chani. What if he is out there? What if he needs Kip's assistance? Then all of his guilt comes flooding back to him. All those victims are not just faceless people; they are friends like Chani, stars like the False Knight. He has no choice in helping them, or else he isn't worthy enough to be holding her hand in the first place.

Stealthily, he finally manages to slip his hand out from hers.

A shiver comes over him from where he was pressed up against her. It isn't as if he doesn't want to stay; he is just frozen with anxiety. He can feel his heart beating—thumping hard against his chest. It feels as though it's going to pop right out of him at any minute.

She stirs slightly. "Don't go, darling," she mumbles in her sleep but doesn't wake. She is peaceful and sweet.

"Damn it," he whispers. That is the name she has for him, and it pains him so to know it.

He turns away from her knowing that he wouldn't be able to sleep ever again unless he did something about the thing causing all the killings topside. For her. Only for her.

Madness

"In the time of man and maniacs, what might seem crazy to some, might also seem perfectly normal to others. Perspectives can be skewed from clouded eyes, or merely turning the other cheek. Normalcy is only biased in that it is rationalized through the absence of information.

"I kill every day and feel nothing for my victims. Sometimes they seem sad, other times devoid of anything. Facing your darkest dragons doesn't automatically make you a legend, nor does bowing to one make you cultist. It's the feelings instilled inside your ill intentions that mold your fate. Sometimes even beauty has an ugly side rearing out of the shadows.

"Only time can play the role of justice in the staleness of death." -*Igon, the Farmer, age 65*

Day Three, 4:39 am: The Change

Cowering in the shadow of the being who just single-handedly took an entire castle without the aid of an army or siege warfare, Kip is more than unnerved. He is traumatized with fear and anticipation. Something about this situation is familiar, like a rhyme at the end of a poet's verse where he knows what is coming next by judging the previous line.

No, he isn't mistaken; he has been in this exact situation before. Why can't he place it in his mind?

There is a fogginess that is impossible to overcome, like a dream he is frantically trying to get back after waking up. This numbed feeling is an old friend—some part of his past that he cannot place for the life of him. Something vague starts to come to his feeble mind...

***

Before becoming quite close, Kip knew the acquaintance he normally traveled to the fair with only as a charity case. That was until destiny sent them on a mission bigger than themselves. Together, they sought to save a forest, a legacy, and a whole bloodline of the feathery bark people. Secrets and past misdeeds clouded the truth among the lies and history of the ancients.

The only thing Kip knew for sure was right from wrong. He was righteous in his quest for liberation of the truth, and anyone who stood in his way must be a villain hellbent on wrongdoings. Back then, he thought that was going to be enough to prevail. Oh, how naive he was.

It was during their quest that Kip recalls one incident in particular. They had approached the underbelly of the old world, seeking the refugees that were held captive, dormant, and still. There was only one problem—the jailer, if you could call him that. His grotesque features made him resemble a beast more than a man, a half-rotted thing that was closer to death than to being alive.

They walked in on the old man eating some awful-smelling meat right off the floor like the animal he had become.

The beast came at them slow and refined, like a demon crawling out of the depths of hell, one dragging foot at a time.

"I warn you. Don't come any closer, fiend," Kip demanded with a just voice, but he was only met with a moist look of discontent.

Even with a third adventurer—a power warrior—by their side, the beast casually made its approach with unwavering confidence. It had nothing to fear, because it was fear itself, hiding its face with a partial mask to spare everyone the full extent of the gnarled, disgusting, putridness that encompassed him.

Their party had come both far and wide, and this was the end of the line. Kip knew what this creature was capable of, and he wasn't going to let it devour him or his friends.

"I've been awaiting your arrival," the beast said through foam-lined lips, which were cracked at the edges.

Kip's male companion stepped forward, but Kip stopped him with a blocking arm. "Then you know why we're here?" He readied his fighting stance.

"I do, but you are much too late to the party. I am sorry to inform you that I had to kill them all."

"You don't sound at all sorry," the female feathered-folk warrior chimed in through gritted teeth.

"I had no choice...I was bored. And now there is but one left for me to complete my little collection," the beast said, as he eyed the female in the group hungrily. "And I thank you both so very much for bringing her to me." The beast gave a slight bow if his head to Kip.

Kip was forced to turn his eyes away from the elderly thing, not only because of putrid smell escaping his mouth when he spoke, but also because of the maggots squirming through his hair as he lowered his head.

"We've come for what's ours—well, his—so stand aside," Kip said, without an introduction.

"His? Who is this *he* you speak of?"

Kip fidgeted his toes inside his boots. He gave away too much. Uncomfortably, he waits a beat.

"No matter. You don't have to answer. They always come for me and leave their corpses behind for me to play with," the man-beast said. His scratchy voice was almost as rough as his appearance.

"You had it all, a castle, kingdom, wealth, and it was never enough," Kip said, shaking his head at the audacity of it all.

The female feathered-folk turned to Kip and whispered, "How do you know this...thing?"

"Don't you remember?" Kip started to say, but then questioned himself quickly. The beast had done many horrible things, and if she doesn't know who is, maybe that isn't a bad thing.

Slowly she shook her head side to side, reiterating what she had asked him. She really didn't know the significance of this fight.

"I'll explain later," Kip whispered, with a wave of his hand, though he had no intention of divulging the absolute truth if it was avoidable.

The beast was now less than human, and if it weren't for the broken mask he wore, Kip might have misidentified him as well.

"This ends. I won't let you win. I know your secrets," Kip said, looking at his acquaintance, the half-breed who had even more of an axe to grind than he did.

"The interesting thing about secrets, boy, is that you need someone to tell. A secret without a voice is merely a non-existence," the beast said, his eye socket glowing yellow through the mask's vision.

The half-breed screamed out in terror—though his mind had long since forgotten about this being, his body was all too familiar with what this creature could do.

"I know more than you think, boy."

"I will distract him. Get out of here and keep to the plan," Kip said to his acquaintances while he picked up a square rock with two handles on it, hoping to turn this simple tool into a weapon for smashing.

The female feathered-folk and the half-breed made a break for the next room at the far end of the cavern, leaving Kip alone with the decrepit beast.

This was his moment to shine, and he was determined to not blow it.

Kip walked right up to the unarmed old beast, the rock weapon high above his head. To Kip, this doesn't seem very sportsmanlike, but murder never is. Maybe if it was running away, he would have felt better.

Kip was going to say something divine, like a blessing for the old thing to take with it in the afterlife, but before he could say another word, the elderly thing launched twenty feet in the blink of an eye—stabbing Kip in the shoulder with an unseen blade.

Kip couldn't swallow nor breathe. So much for sportsmanship. One hit was all it took. Kip didn't see where the fencing sword had come from. But it didn't matter; it was there, pressing into him like a pin in a pin cushion.

"What were you thinking? Were you just going to walk up to me and hit me with a rock? Was that your big secret plan?"

"I..." Kip was suddenly weak and dropped the improvised stone weapon backwards. An unbearable sensation coursed through his entire body in his defeat. Glassy-eyed and dumbfounded, Kip's expression went vacant.

"Please tell me there is more. Maybe I was a little too hasty in my assault."

Once the full extent of the injury reached him, his body let out a horrific wail as loud as his voice could carry. Never had he felt such agonizing pain. It was beyond crippling. It was unimaginable to him how anyone could live with such an injury, as small as it seemed. He wanted nothing more than to die right then, and not a second later.

"Quiet down," the beast said, shoving an old rag inside his mouth, muting him somewhat.

Powerless to do anything, he stood there as an object, not as a human being.

"I don't want you to spoil the secret." The beast held a gnarled finger with long yellow nails over his lips. "Shhh."

With every single passing moment, the

immeasurable pain increased exponentially, followed by a deep fear that left him feeling detached from himself.

"Give me your best shot." The beast closed its glowing eye and lowered itself to Kip, leaving its sword unattended, still lodged inside Kip's shoulder. "I could have killed you instantly, but I wanted to do it slowly, because time is the loneliest of all companions."

Every thought, every part of himself was focused on the agony. So much torturous pain. It was something entirely new for him, and it was all-consuming.

"I guess that really was all you had in store for me, then." The beast returned his gaze to his paralyzed combatant. He twisted the sword causing Kip's cry to reach greater heights, even through the dampening effect of the rag in his mouth.

The old beast tried to speak, though his words were lost in the sea of Kip's cries.

Removing the sword caused Kip to instantly drop to the floor, curled up in a ball—his screams turning into loud sobs.

"You're making this unpleasant for me. Can you at least pretend to be a man?"

The fogginess that kept him at bay slowly

dissipated into the back of his mind, and Kip wondered what magic could have caused such a dreadful sensation with such a thin steel blade. Never had he felt such discomfort. It was unbearable, and it poisoned his courage.

"Despicable." The beast raised his sword ready to end Kip's suffering for purely selfish reasons—his ears couldn't take it any longer.

Still reeling from the last hit, all Kip could do was close his eyes tightly and embrace his own demise. With his mind's eye, he hears the foe ready his next attack with a gurgling, grunting sound that was both powerful and gross. This one should be even more devastating than the last. It would all be over in a mere moment.

With a swift lunge, the beast made his final strike. But this time, Kip didn't feel a thing.

Was that blow so efficient that he died instantly? A merciful death? He slowly opened his eyes and saw a figure standing between himself and the monster.

She had blocked his attack with her outstretched arm, letting it go right through her body. Yet she wasn't crying; she didn't even seem to be affected...

"You didn't think I would leave a fight this easily, did you?" the feathered-folk woman said, kicking the old bastard to the floor while simultaneously disarming him of his weapon...

***

That memory was the first time Kip found his fear. It wasn't some great spell or magical effect. It was a normal amount of agony for an exceptionally weak being. Everything in his world has changed since that day.

Seeing Kip face to face with the embodiment of evil as it charges up an attack, a small pod of victims uses this opportunity to flee.

This catches the robed-figure's attention, and he points his hand in their direction instead.

Energy projectiles manifest out of his glowing hand and take to the air. His ominous stride is chilling as he walks slowly towards the group, now ignoring Kip—as if he knows that he isn't going anywhere.

Day Two, 11:11 pm: A Long-Lost Lie

What Kip isn't is heroic, brave, or anything special. At least that's how he feels about himself. When push comes to shove, he always finds himself on the ground. It's nearly impossible to really see your own virtues when you're always looking outward. Yes, he isn't tall, particularly strong, or any of the conventional traits one associates with a hero. The truth is that true heroism isn't a look or a chiseled smile; it is built upon actions alone. They are reserved for people who stand up for those weaker and less capable than themselves. That is who you look up to, not the egocentric boasters that take all the credit when the smoke settles.

Kip doesn't see it that way though. He likes the fantasy of it all. Good conquers evil and always triumphs in the end. This statement is less true than anyone would like to admit. Comfort comes in hope.

If he cannot believe in himself, Kip has to have faith in the band of brave warriors. They are the ones who are putting their lives on the line to fight against unspeakable odds.

In comparison, Kip feels that he's only doing a fraidy-cat's work under the comfortable guise of a champion. So badly does he want to be like the Conductor Knight, previously known as the False Knight. There was nothing false about his sacrifice, and so Kip came up with a more fitting name to remember him by.

Romanticizing about his own storybook ending, Kip would love to give his life for others. Instead, this is the best he can do—just short of giving up.

In the backdrop of the fallen casualties, warriors fight valiantly against the unknown foe deeper in the castle. Kip knows the threat is close to them, much too close for his liking. Still, they carry on as they continue launching scattered arrows, charging swords, and chopping axes. As a single unit, they are fighting for their lives and the lives of many fallen on the ground.

In the midst of the turmoil, Kip helps a limping youth by placing his arm over his shoulder.

"I got it. Go help someone worse off than I am," the youth says.

"Are you sure?"

"Just point me in the right direction."

Kip extends a shaky finger at the candlelight flickering from a nearby alcove. "It is just over there." Without missing a beat, Kip tosses a child over his shoulder. "Follow me."

Snapping out of shock, the kid starts to scream and kick Kip as he races to the triage area.

All the commotion of the child throws Kip off balance, and he trips over a corpse.

The child takes off into an alcove.

"I don't have time to chase you. Please find shelter. It is safe right over there," Kip says, making sure he himself isn't hurt.

After everything seems to be in working order, he returns to victims less fortunate than the child, just in time to see the limping youth get hit by a wild crossbow bolt, dropping him to the floor. This is another danger of being out on the battlefield. There is so much going on in the mass confusion of things that sometimes there are casualties from friendly fire.

Jumping over several human mounds, Kip makes it over to the youth who was nearly at his destination before he fell. "Now you're less fortunate."

"I think you're right," the youth says with a chuckle, trying to hide his discomfort.

Kip tries to pick him up, but the pain is too much for the youth to bear.

"I can't at the moment. Leave me. Go save someone else."

"You tried to get rid of me once already." Telling him to let him die is just the sort of virtue that Kip deems worthy of his attention, no matter how long it takes. "I'll be right back."

Taking off like a leaf in the wind, Kip makes his way back to the triage area, where he spies several healing circles. This is a method where the wounded are lying shoulder to shoulder in a circle around a witch doctor, or some other healer of sorts. There are dozens of these circles, and they are a great tactic to allow the healers to treat many wounded without having to venture off too far.

"Salm oil...do you have any?" Kip asks the healer in the closest circle to him.

The bell healer looks at Kip as if he is speaking another language and continues ringing his cleansing bells.

It is possible that he doesn't understand the common tongue that Kip has taken for granted. That, or maybe he doesn't like the distraction to his treatment song.

The healer at circle directly to the right of him is busy removing two dead bodies and replacing them with fresh mortally wounded.

Things are a little hectic at the moment inside the triage area.

Without thinking, Kip starts to drink from a helmet filled with water that a helper shoves in his face. Helpers are everywhere and giving the healers aid to any task necessary. Kip is so parched that he doesn't even notice nor care that the helmet doesn't appear to be at all sanitary.

A godless pagan priest rushes to Kip, "I have some I can spare. Here, take it," she says, obviously having heard Kip's initial request.

Her generosity is contrary to what the people of his homeland have to say about the pagan faith, but there isn't time for him to dwell on religious beliefs. She is helping, and he is appreciative.

Before he can finish drinking, Kip snatches the root out of the priest's hand and bounds back towards where he left the wounded youth. "Thanks!" Kip yells back in the direction of the triage area. He is so determined to reach the youth that he almost forgot to thank her. It is most likely that she didn't even hear him, but what really matters is that he said it—as long as an omniscient being heard him.

Sliding to a quick stop, Kip reaches the youth with the healing root in hand. Oil of a salm root is a remedy his mother always used to treat his wounds, even when he was younger than this injured youth before him. It's a miracle substance with healing properties that are astounding, if Kip's memory serves him correctly.

On the ground, Kip procures himself a broken edge of a weapon. Once he braces the root against the ground, he quickly starts to shave off the outer layer of the root, allowing the oil to be squeezed out.

"What's that you're doing there?" the youth asks, grabbing his side.

"It will heal you. It is a miracle medicine called salm."

"I don't want it."

"Why not? It will help you with the pain and clotting."

"Salm oil has no healing properties whatsoever."

"That is nonsense. Here, take it." Kip holds the root up.

"No. I don't want it."

"Why in blazes not?"

"It's a narcotic. The bad kind."

"Nonsense," Kip says, wiping the drop of oil on his index finger and bringing it up to his own lips.

"All it does is make you forget your pain. It doesn't help you heal."

"No. I don't believe you."

"It's true. It's a powerful memory blocker," another person on the ground chimes in. "My whole town was once addicted to salm, and it took an outside source to intervene for us to get off the stuff. It's really dangerous, if you ask me."

"Well, no one asked you." True or not, Kip feels stupid for offering the stuff to the youth. He isn't trying to push an addictive substance on anyone; he is only trying to help.

Suddenly Kip starts to feel in a daze as the truth starts to sink in, despite him not wanting it to.

Events of his past rush through his foggy memory. All throughout his life, he remembers being administered the oil, but he can't for the life of him remember what happened directly after taking it. Also, he can't remember why he needed the healing medicine in the first place.

Kip places his head inside his palm. This is a hard one for him to grasp, but deep down, he knows there is something not quite right about his past and how he is remembering it. He tries to focus hard on those particular missing moments, but all he sees is blackness. It is as if the memory is masked, or it has simply been erased.

If what they are saying is true, has he been fed a lie to cope with pain his entire life? This might explain why he never remembers the act that made him a childhood hero in his hometown. Over and over again, he has heard the tale, but he can never quite picture it. Maybe he was fearless in that moment because he had never recalled fear and the consequences of his actions before, or perhaps it is far worse...perhaps it never really happened at all.

Could his mother, family, and friends all be in on a sick joke at his expense? *How far would they go to perpetuate a lie?* As far as necessary, now he realizes. Back home, he is quite cared for, nearly coddled. Their love and affection towards him are what drove him to leave home in the first place. He wanted to make it on his own, and as long as they were around, he wouldn't be able to.

Wait, that isn't right. He has told this shore story so many times, he now believes it himself. *Why did I really leave?*

Unfortunately, leaving the easy life has left him ill-equipped for the tarnished lands set before him, and this day is by far the worst he has ever experienced. Never in his wildest nightmares did he ever expect to see such desolation and anguish.

Defeated, Kip slumps down next to the wounded youth, giving in to the possibility of it all. "Are you absolutely sure?"

"I'm afraid I am."

You cannot change who you are. Who am I kidding? Heroes are not made—they're born and bred that way. Greatness cannot be taught. It's only given to those worthy of it. And I always fall short no matter how hard I try. So why bother at all?

He feels as though the answer is at the tip of his tongue and on the cusp of his mind, but it won't come to him. Maybe it was blacked out like the rest of his life. Or maybe he hasn't learned that lesson yet.

Day Three, 4:42 am: A Statue of Flesh

Motionless in the devastated arena, the immoral being leaves Kip behind like some leftovers on a plate from a particularly unappetizing meal. Will it be back to clear off what little remains? Well, that depends on its hunger for death. The thing doesn't seem to be lacking many targets at the moment.

Numbness overcomes Kip completely, leaving him nothing more than a shell of a person—devoid of movement or action. There he stands with the same frozen expression of terror he had when he thought his life was about to cease. Fearing everything, his mind is just as paralyzed as the rest of him, like a portrait capturing a moment in space and time—a living piece of art rife with the emotion off foreboding on his face.

Slowly and steadily, the slaughter moves farther away from him until it is completely out of earshot. And with the quietness of the morning, Kip feels almost safe. Yet he remains standing without moving a single muscle. He is breathing, but the rising and falling movements of his chest escape his consciousness. It is as if his spirit left his body prematurely and the rest of him is wondering why it can't follow.

As the minutes blur into hours, nothing is left but the lonely chill of defeat.

Off in the distance, something is scurrying around, breaking in and out of the shadows the spot fires are casting.

All of Kip's muscles tense and lock up. This is the moment he realizes that they were once relaxed. Even having that thought is proof that he is slowly coming out of his comatose state. It isn't every day that you come face-to-face with a god and live to tell about it—although the day is young, and this isn't over yet.

The scurrying sound is getting closer. Could it be the all-powerful one that put him in this state? No, it is much too small for that. *Maybe it's in a different form—like a shifter.* His ears perk up trying to discern what it is. A mouse or house cat, maybe? Whatever it is, it's nearly upon him now.

Based on its meek movements, this creature is a scavenger, not a ruthless killer. This gives him a little solace.

Kip tries to shoo the thing away with a threatening sound, but his face doesn't move. Instead, a hissing sound of air leaks out of his agape lips.

Small clawed hands start to pull back his leggings.

He knows something is there, but the cold of the morning has made him void of all feeling in his body. There is only a strong tingling and fairly detached feeling.

The sound of chomping teeth and tearing flesh paint a horrific picture in Kip's mind. He is being eaten alive, and he feels nothing in the form of pain from it.

No. No, no, no. I can't just let this happen. I don't want to be remembered this way.

Kip instantly has control over himself again, as if he were just brought into this world. Confused and wet with the morning dew, he flails his limbs violently with the animated movements of a baby being born.

The little beast is knocked back a couple feet and gobbles up the morsel of him it has in its mouth. Growling and baring its tiny fangs is a rodent-sized dog. Much smaller than a fox but also slightly larger than a rat, it has an elongated, pointy snout accommodating quite a lot of teeth. It would almost be cute if it hadn't just eaten a chunk of him.

"Hey! Get out of here. I'm not dead...not yet!" Kip yells, trying to scare away the menace. As he says the words, he realizes that maybe that's why it chose to gnaw on him instead of the hundreds if not thousands of corpses all around the castle. It must like warm flesh.

The more he taunts the thing, the more it screeches at him in a high-pitched, drawn-out bark.

All he can do is kick and swipe at the little

beast to keep it at bay.

The dog-rat dodges and weaves, only to double back and lap up some splattered blood from his motions.

Looking down, Kip realizes that his blood is flowing into his boot. At this rate he's going to bleed out if he doesn't stop it. This little bastard really got him good.

In general, Kip has a lot of affinity towards animals, but he is going to have to overcome those warm fuzzy feelings if he doesn't want to be its lunch.

He raises his leg to stomp this critter into the next life when he hears even more scurrying off in the distance.

It opens its maw and catches each drop of blood from his raised leg.

To the left and right of Kip appear dozens more of these tiny dogs. They must have heard this one's little cry.

At first, he might have thought this one was a puppy or juvenile, but after seeing more of them, it has to be an adult. This is not good.

Changing tactics, Kip opts to kick the thing towards the incoming threat instead of squashing it like a fever grub. If anything, it might be a good enough distraction for him to make a break for it.

About thirty feet away, the thing lands hard, but abruptly stands on its hind legs, giving Kip a threatening snarl.

Now it's angry.

Half surrounded, Kip doesn't know what to do. The pack of little dogs licks their chops at the sight of him scared and defenseless.

The blood-faced one he kicked starts to limp over towards Kip again, not giving up.

"This thing is relentless."

Unexpectedly, the newly arrived rodent-dogs pounce on the wounded one, noticing its wounded stride—tearing it apart one bite at a time. They are ravenous.

Kip watches in revulsion as he witnesses what those little beasts are capable of. The one on him was nothing compared to the awfulness of the rest of the pack.

This is his opportunity to flee, and he almost squanders it. But he does run—like a wounded rabbit from a pack of starving foxes.

A Warning of a Threat

"If only I had more time.
"More toys at my disposal.
"More evil to kill.
"More girls to impress.
"More words to say.
"And most of all, more blood to bleed..."
-*"Landy the Page, age 13.*

Day One, 12:33 pm: Prediction

Kip wonders what about his booth is so unappealing. Not that he is exactly keeping track, but it seems as though every other vendor has a lot more foot traffic, sales, and general interest than he does. Vouchers and merchandise are changing hands left and right, although no action is happening around his table. It's just him and his weeds, both looking equally sad.

Person after person pass by his setup without a second glance. One woman even pulls her child in to her side in a protective sort of move. He wonders if it's him. *Do I have the wrong attitude?* Or maybe having negative thoughts are yielding him negative results, like some sort of mind-over-matter thing.

Maybe this crowd just isn't at all interested in plants and germination, he contemplates. They do seem to be more city-like folk with their fancy hats and garb. In the beginning, this event started out as a local farming harvest festival, and now it has evolved into something much broader.

Kip quickly touches his face, hoping he hadn't forgotten to wipe the red sauce from his lunch of cabbage and meat stew. No, it wasn't that.

He spies a customer who just bought a pile of parchments from the anti-social scroll seller to his right.

The customer is a nicely dressed youth and is having a pleasant conversation about cooking and the science behind love potions.

This isn't at all fair. Kip tried to start a conversation with the scroll smith many times and was only met with grunts and moans. This is the first sign that the scroll smith can actually speak, and it looks like that greatest conversation Kip has ever not been a part of.

After a bit, the youth waves goodbye and heads on down the line. Before buying scrolls, he was getting some good luck crystals from the vendor two tables down. And before that, he was doing something at the table even further down the way. This is a perfect customer, one that goes down the line and buys something from everyone, and now it's Kip's turn.

He waits with eager delight. Kip is certain this is his shot, if not for a sale, at least for a great conversation. Except, the customer noticeably avoids Kip's booth altogether. His joyful smile turns into an unapproachable frown.

There goes another one.

To make matters worse, the customer pulls out some coin vouchers to buy some explosives from the seller on his left, Sarl.

Is he really going to buy something from everyone else but me?

There has to be something Kip's doing that is putting people off. There is no way that it is just in his imagination. He scribbles down a list of possible reasons on some sample parchment that blew off his neighbor's table.

1. The script on my sign is too good, and I seem like some sort of elite.

2. I didn't dress festive enough and therefore come across as sourpuss.

3. Wrong market.

4. Poor location, with bad visibility.

Kip takes a moment to reflect on his booth this year, which is much better than the previous year's spot—hidden behind a kite and wind sock salesman.

4. The customers are friends or have established relationships with the vendors.

5. It is slow or far too early.

6. I am a horrible seller.

"Well, how can I expect to make a sale when no one comes up to me?" Kip argues with his list as if it's a person capable of cognitive debate.

7. There are rumors about me.

8. Everyone is broke.

"No, people are handing over vouchers left and right."

9. Our mission is complete, and there are no more materials in these parts.

"Why did I write that down? I know for a fact that's not true." But he keeps it on the list anyway as it might be a relevant reason at some later point for him to look back on. Paper is hard to come by in this deforested area, so he has to come up with ways to make good use of every piece he gets before ultimately turning it into wiping sheets.

10. My prices are far too low/high.

After mulling over the list a couple of times, he comes to the conclusion that maybe it is his lack of engagement with the customers passing by.

Taking the initiative, he decides that maybe he should be standing instead of sitting. It might make him look less bored and more ap-proachable.

Somehow taking to his feet causes him to be colder. He has to stop the urge to pace back and forth. The other problem is that now Kip doesn't know where to put his arms so that they don't make him feel awkward. He tries to place both hands behind his head, but that is way too forward, and people keep looking at his belly peeking out of the gap in his shirt. "Too confident."

Switching to crossing his arms makes him feel like he appears to be angry. He tries to counter that by raising his eyebrows, only now he looks insane. Finally, he places one arm on his hip like the handle of a teapot. A man walks by and whistles at Kip in a cat-call sort of way. Or at least he thinks it's directed towards him, but he kind of hopes it wasn't. Somehow this pose is a little too flirtatious for his liking.

That's it. I have to move. Kip rubs his hands together and blows into them for warmth.

The next person making an approach is a wealthy-looking man with a clean shave and crisp evening attire. By the time Kip gets around the table, the man has already started to veer away towards the dense traffic in the center of the cobblestone street.

Walking is proving to be a great way to hide his arm positions. It takes a little double step, but Kip is now successfully blocking the man's path and has his full attention.

"Hello, sir, can I help you with anything?"

The wealthy man looks as though Kip is mistaken with the placement of his looming look. He points at himself to make sure he wasn't reading the stare incorrectly.

"Yes, you. I am talking to you. Let me start again. Hello." Kip motions for the man to reposition his route towards the Seeds and Weeds table.

Reluctantly, the man takes a couple steps closer. "Do I know you?" he asks.

"Well, not exactly, but I would love to talk to you about indigenous agriculture in this area."

"No chance. I'm just here for the milk wine and food." The man turns away quickly.

Instincts urge Kip to tuck tail and return to the comfort of behind his table, but success is stepping out of your comfort zone, no matter how uncomfortable it may be. So, he persists at the risk of coming across as pushy. "I am paying top tickets for any of these specifically." Kip holds up the only pit he has acquired during the first hours of the faire.

"I said I'm not interested!" The man takes another turn, this time making his way straight towards Kip's table.

With a slight tip of his head, Kip wonders why the man's actions are directly contrary to his words. Maybe he doesn't realize that it is where Kip was trying to get him to go. Either way, he is determined and isn't going to give up that easily. *What do I have to lose? A sale? Highly doubtful.*

Ignoring the cues, Kip continues on with his pitch, "You know, most people think that I am in the market for selling wares, but I am actually here looking to buy." Fixated and not taking his eyes off the man, Kip sees some sort of crazed stare starting to develop in the man's eyes.

After seeing that look, maybe he should let this one pass but he's in way too deep now, so he carries on. "I am in the market for seeds—or pits, as they are often referred to. Let me ask you, have you seen any of these before?" Kip holds up the sample in his grasp.

Without even a single glance, the man's face is now red hot like a raging bull.

Regret comes in hard and fast. This might have been a horrible mistake. Kip cringes and covers his face, thinking a beating is unavoidable.

Out of the crowd, a passerby stumbles in between them. "You guys look tense."

Kip opens his squinting eyes upon hearing

anything other than the sound of himself getting pummeled. After a double-take, he looks directly at the passerby. The middle-aged man has unkempt blond hair that is matted and greasy. He wears a matching set of tattered clothes, which was obviously pilfered from a trash pile. The first thought that comes to mind is that this person must have snuck into the event like a gatecrasher—unable to pay the entry fee.

The surge of hope Kip had for a peaceful resolution is quickly gone. Through a sideways glance, he notices that the wealthy man has both his fists clenched tightly ready to strike. He wasn't misreading things—a fight was exactly where this encounter was leading.

"Hey, let's not fight among ourselves. There isn't time for such petty things," the newcomer says in a calming voice—monotone and relaxed.

"This affair doesn't concern you, vagrant. This matter is between my fists and his face," the wealthy man says, as if he is annoyed by the delay. After getting a whiff of Kip's savior, who has the sweaty smell of alcohol as if it is perfume, he asks, "Did I say vagrant? I mean drunkard." The wealthy man waves his hand across his face in an attempt to fan away the stench.

The fact that one of his fists is now un-clenched doesn't escape Kip. *One down, one to go.* With a little luck, there is a chance of defusing this whole misunderstanding, if that's what it is. "Don't judge, you said yourself that you came here for drinks. Milk wine, was it?" The words fall out of Kip before he has a chance to think them. It's strange how he can't for the life of him stand up for himself, but once the wealthy man starts to treat the vagrant poorly, he finally finds his courage.

"Do you two know each other?" the wealthy man asks with an accusatory finger.

The vagrant drunkard and Kip both eye each other, slowly shaking their perspective heads back and forth, denying the accusation.

"Then get out of my way, you filthy rat." With a slight shove, the wealthy man is now nose-to-nose with Kip.

"We are all going to die soon enough. The darkness is coming. For you, me, all of this, and all of us. We are all the same in death's rotten eye," the vagrant says, slurring through his words with an almost gleeful undertone.

Kip realizes that his savior isn't merely

drunk, but he has also lost his mind. *He proba-bly drinks to disarm all the voices in his head.*

"That's a good one! Darkness, death's eye...what other predictions did you find in the garbage pile?" The wealthy man turns all his rage into a bellyful of uproarious laughter—taking a couple generous steps backwards.

This is either a wonderful distraction or ramblings from an unhinged individual. At any rate, it is working. Kip is now out of arm's length. The wealthy man's hands are no longer fists, and he seems much less angry about the whole thing.

"This is no joke. It is a forewarning, a prem-onition of things to be. You can't stop it—no one can. We must all leave before it's far too late," the vagrant says, grabbing the wealthy man's finely crafted night coat.

If he wanted to calm things down, laying hands on the wealthy man isn't the best idea, even Kip knows that. This must mean that it isn't a well-thought-out tactic. He must really believe his words to be truth.

"Really? If it is as serious as you make it sound, then why are you smiling?" the wealthy man asks flatly. Without waiting for a response and with two snaps of his fingers, a couple of goons come out of nowhere and immediately flank them. "This guy has to go. He is bothering me."

The goons grab the vagrant under his arms and proceed to eject him from the area, without another word from the wealthy man.

"This is not a threat. It's the trut..." the vagrant yells but receives a punch to the stomach for raising his voice.

"Hey, you can't do that. He obviously isn't right in the head. You're hurting him!" Kip tries to reason with the wealthy man, the goons...really anyone who will listen, but it is no use. What's done is already done.

He looks left and then right, but there are no guards or anyone around to help the poor vagrant. Kip feels his hand touch the dagger by his side in a natural sort of way, but the moment quickly passes uneventfully.

The wealthy man shakes his head back and forth while making his way to the closest tavern. Many patrons have migrated around the outside of the establishment due to overcrowding.

Something seems off. Everything the vagrant said seemed so farfetched. But if that is true, why does Kip feel as if something very important is about to happen? Dumbfounded, he stands there motionless, waiting, but nothing changes. People are still eating, walking, talking, dancing, drinking, and carrying on as always.

He jolts himself around, thinking the sense is coming from behind him somehow, but there is nothing there.

Should I be so quick to discount the vagrant's warning? Yes. He is clearly drunk. This is all inside my head. Look at how happy everyone is, Kip reasons with himself, like he always does when fear gets the better of him.

And just like that, the feeling in his gut goes away...but not forever.

Day Three, 11:04 am: One Thing Left to Resolve

Without the will to carry on, the inspiration to fight, or the ingenuity to come up with any ideas, Kip is left with nothing but the constant sound of destruction haunting him, wearing on his conscious.

His face twitches and contorts upon feeling the pain from his past injuries flare up. Every part of his body is left in misery. He quickly rummages through his bag, but it's empty, just like it was an hour ago, and an hour before that. For some reason, he thought that this time it would be different and filled with the very thing he craves.

After wrapping his hurt leg, the weight of the events really starts to sink in. Every death pushes down on him, visibly making his body seem almost squashed.

With each burst or loud booming noise, he imagines another life leaving this realm forever. He wonders why he can't be so lucky. For it all to be over would be a blissful state. Whatever that thing is, it's unstoppable, he knows. So, what is the point of waiting for it to escort him to the afterlife?

His mind goes around and around in circles until he is mentally dizzy. *Why is this happening to me? Why can't I face what needs to be done?* He wonders why so many lives have been lost without even trying, and why has he been spared? Kip doesn't want to be spared, though. He is too insignificant to face the thing. He tried, and it left him even more broken than before. He doesn't want to hurt anymore. He wants it all to end.

He pulls off a sturdy-looking tablecloth that

is resting on a nearby table. Burying his teeth into the cloth to get it started, he shreds it into thin strips. Kip's busy hands fiddle with the cloth as he tries to distract himself from the events of the past few days.

If the wizard cannot be stopped, this must be the end of the world, the end of it all. Suddenly his whole mission and goals seem quite trivial in the grand scheme of things. He feels insignificant and lower than he ever has before. "What is the point of anything anymore?" He wants nothing more than to control the emotions that are running rampant within him, but he can't.

Without aforethought, his hands craft him an unknowing solution—they tie a noose with the strips of tablecloth that ironically were made to protect whatever they cover from harm.

Anything is better than this, he believes, and quickly slips the noose around his neck with as much care as if it were a magical neckpiece.

This is his only way out, a fitting death for a waste such as himself. Now he has enough motivation to stand, to move about and look for a rafter, or anything high enough to hang the other end of the fabric rope from.

His heart is racing as he makes his way to the center of the castle's kitchen. There, he spies the perfect setting for his end. The sky shines through a hole in the ceiling used as a vent that was built to let all the smoke escape. A custom pig-roasting apparatus is just high enough for his legs to dangle off the ground, though easy enough to access. He tosses the braided fabric over the pig roaster, then quickly ties it off and finally makes his way to the edge of table. This is it—the end. His end.

Reflecting on the wonders of his life, he pauses before leaping to his self-inflicted death. He feels at peace with his decision, almost tranquilly so. For the first time since this whole thing started, he has control over his actions and his life. He doesn't have to endure any more throbbing pain. In a moment, it will all be over.

Moisture fills his eyes as he looks back on who he has become, where the only escape from his pain is to embrace his own end.

The irony is that his fear of getting murdered from the wizard is pushing him to jump to his own demise, where each one ultimately leads to the very same end. Unfortunately, the hard truth is that this is the easier way out. All he has to do is take a step. Fighting that monster is a much, much harder thing to face. It is hours, if not days, of suffering to endure. He has already had as much as he can stand. This is the only way.

His foot teeters at the edge of the slick table. Just one more step to go.

Then something unexpected happens. Kip feels a small tug on the end of his shirt. Startled, he spins around, almost losing his footing and falling off the table. For the moment, his will to survive is fueled by his desire to see what is bothering him so. He waves and flails his arms wildly to try and keep his balance.

Once stable, he looks down at a young boy standing next to the table.

"What do you need? I am a little busy right now," Kip asks, greatly agitated, using his arm to hide the suicidal rope around his neck.

"Oh, I am sorry. I just wanted to ask you something is all."

"Go ahead," Kip sighs slightly.

"Are you going to make yourself die?"

"Look, I have my own reasons. Don't try and talk me out of it," Kip says, dropping his arms, knowing the jig is up.

"No, I wasn't going to ask you that."

"What, then?"

"Can I please be next?"

Kip looks deeply into the boy's wide eyes and can't help but feel a pang a sympathy for the kid. How can someone so courteous and young be concerned with such things as putting an end to his own life? Surely this youngling didn't go through anything like Kip has in the last day and a half. But that thought is fleeting. Perhaps he saw far worse…

"What? No, you most definitely may not. Find your own way. This one is mine." Seeing the innocence inside the kid's broken soul causes a sadness to come over Kip, and for a moment he sees himself inside those big eyes. Instantly he doesn't feel so alone.

"You don't need his permission. Just take it off his corpse. That is what I plan on doing," another young boy around the same age admits from his hiding place.

"You most certainly will not." Kip starts to remove the noose from his neck and untie the end. This is not how he ever imagined inspiring others. "I've changed my mind. You will all have to wait to die like everyone else." Hand over hand, he pulls the fabric rope down from the pig roaster. The end flops over with a thud like the body of a dead snake.

The two boys look at Kip with slack-jawed expressions.

"That isn't at all fair," the younger one says.

"Yeah, where do you get off?" someone else chimes in.

"I'm not saying you can't die. It's your right, but just not now and not with my rope," Kip says sternly. He is okay with having his own death on his conscious but knowing that he helped others' is something he can't live with, even if it is just for the couple of seconds leading up to his own suicide.

Out of nowhere, more people join in the ruckus and start to pull and fight over the noose Kip has created—shoving him out of the way. There are more people inside this room than Kip ever expected.

"If you're not going to do it, give it here!" one person says.

"Hey, I was next," another voice says.

They start to argue with each other on the fairness of who gets a turn at killing themselves with the noose. It's like watching kids fight over a toy and who gets to play with it first—except their ages are all over the place, from about seven to fifty.

Kip looks over to see a man in chef's attire holding a freshly cooked meal. Steam fills the room, and its scent confirms what Kip's eyes have already guessed. It is surely delicious, too. A meal fit for a king. Maybe it *was* for a king. Who knows? But it is a three-course meal with all the fixings, either way.

Kip wonders what could have happened to convince someone to cooking a meal like that in a time like this but quickly brushes off his musing. There are more pressing matters to deal with currently—for starters, his precious fabric rope.

In this morbid moment, Kip sees the fight he has inspired from a positive angle. Sure, at first it started as a means to put an end to all of their lives. But now they are doing something besides waiting for death.

"Give me my noose back!" Kip commands with a mighty roar.

The room falls silent, and he snatches up his belonging. It is shredded beyond repair. They ruined it.

In a way, this whole incident has given Kip another perspective on himself, one he couldn't see objectively while wallowing in self-doubt. He gains a renewed outlook, one in which giving up is no longer an option. Not for him. Not for anyone.

Day Four, 3:40 pm: Immortal Memory

Upon seeing the wizard, Kip knows he has been in this exact situation before, but he cannot recall right away.

The eyes and the teeth are different, but the body is positively the same. He starts to remember the arena. The grand murderer left him standing still for an unknown amount of time. *How could I have forgotten that? Or is it a false memory?*

It could have been a day ago, or a month, even a year. All his thoughts are garbled up and reorganizing themselves in a strange order.

As the Wizard slowly glides closer to him, he starts to feel a forgotten feeling, something he thought to have eradicated hours, if not days, ago.

It's the return of his weakness—dreadful pain. Sitting in the shadow of the wizard is crippling. Just being near him causes all Kip's bones and muscles to ache. It is his sensitivity to the pain that really has a hold on him. There is so much energy radiating off his body that even his shadow feels warm to the touch. *A special occasion. That's right. I was celebrating something. Or someone?*

Then the truth hits him like a devastating blow to the head with a two-handed maul. The root...he must have taken the numbing root. Someone warned him about the narcotic. Who was it...? The wounded youth. But Kip didn't believe him. Or perhaps he did, and that's the true reason he ingested it. No, it is something far worse, something he can't truly confront.

That is the only reasonable answer to all his questions. That's why he can't feel or remember everything. His mind is more scrambled than an egg. He must have had his reasons for taking the stuff, but unfortunately for him, it's beginning to wear off, and so is his confidence.

I must have seen or felt something really bad to want to take the root. But what is worse than everything I do remember? Why did I give in to it? I knew the effects, yet I took it anyway. I had to have had my reasons. How long has this been taking effect?

Sizing himself up, Kip looks for any injuries he cannot account for.

Tiny dog bite, rope burn, bruised, dragged, kicked by a goat, skewered, cut on his hand, banged, and burned. Everything seems to be accounted for. *Wait. When did I cut my hand?*

That is the one injury that is missing from his memory. It's a tiny scratch. Surely he wouldn't have taken the salm root for something so small. No matter how hard he tries, he cannot recall exactly where he got that cut from.

The real danger is that Kip is once again up against a foe he has no place fighting. He isn't a murderer...

Then a glint of the memory comes back to him. He sees the face of the man he blindly stabbed through the throat.

No. He isn't that person. Never would he kill someone. It isn't in his power to commit that level of harm to someone. A heavy feeling comes over him. The tiny cut must have been from the double-bladed dagger during the act of his throw. That is why the widow wouldn't let go of his hand; she was applying pressure to his wound to keep it from bleeding.

Why did he have to remember? He doesn't want to think of himself as being a bad guy. How can he live with himself knowing that he took a life, even if it was by accident. Or was it? The fog wasn't quite as solid as he had previously remembered. He could see the shape of two silhouettes struggling against each other. The man pulled back his arm to slap the woman, and that's when he threw the thing...hard.

Life has a way of repeating itself if a lesson is not learned. It gives a constant reminder of exactly how delicate and small everyone really is.

Before he had the encounter with the beast in the old world, Kip thought of himself as strong—a little small in stature, sure, but a hero type true and true. The only problem was that no one else saw the internal strength he felt he had all along. He had decided that if they wouldn't take his word for it, he would let his actions speak for him. Only, he didn't like what his actions were saying.

This is the third time in his life that he is face-to-face with a horrible creature of great importance. *What does it all mean?*

He is so entranced with his thoughts that he almost forgets about the dangerous being coming straight for him.

If this is my time, so be it. I cannot stop it anymore than I can stop him from killing anyone else. But if I want a chance, I have to follow the clues, now more than ever.

Closing his eyes, Kip tries hard to recall every detail about the first time he found pain and defeat. There is something important about that moment, and he isn't grasping it. This time he must remember all their names, in order to remember himself.

The female feathered-folk. No...she has a name...Lisa? No, that's too human of a name. I am sure that it starts with the letter "L." Lllllancer. Yes, Lancer is her name. Something happened to her. She was somehow different than I remembered her. I used to stare at it. I couldn't help myself. But what was it?

Damn, I can't picture it. Remembering the exact details is important for his sanity—to reverse the effects of the root, if that's even possible. But he has to try and make sense of everything.

I was on edge before we found her, for some reason.

Having Lancer next to him made Kip feel invincible. There is something about being part of a winning team, where undeserved pride bolsters you up. And Kip was no exception. When she was around, he was bigger than himself—

more confident and self-assured. But nothing could have prepared him for what was to come...finding the old lord in a secluded cave.

Yes, that's where the immortal beast was hidden, inside a decrepit exterior shell and almost unrecognizable. *But I knew him, somehow, and I hated him. He was the only person I've*

ever truly hated. That means the beast could only be Lord Neff.

"You came back," the old lord had said to Lancer from his ground position after she kicked him.

"Did you miss me?" Lancer responded with a smirk.

If she had known it was Neff, she might not have been so brazen. That may have been a blessing. Kip envied her ignorance.

A pang of disgust had come over him when he recalled the previous time he had seen the lord—through the effects of the Pit of the Forest, a magical relic with wonderous powers. This time, the Lord was far less than his former glory, especially in how slowly he moved. He was less of a man and more of a creature than anything. That must be why he referred to him as a beast.

"I've been watching you all on this little es-cape," the old lord had said, balancing on his knee to rise to his hunched-over posture.

The mask, he still has it on. It must be work-ing, Kip recalls thinking.

"That is a fair bit creepy," Lancer said.

"I...don't care about you, or your little games. Let us take the...pits, and we will be on our way," Kip interjected, managing to muster up a complete sentence through the throbbing pain in his shoulder from a deep cut.

"You know I cannot do that. You will build an army against me. Just like last time."

Lancer had looked at Kip as if she was going to mentally berate him later on about this new-found information.

"You're old. Do the right thing and let us pass without quarrel," Kip demanded.

"I don't know who you think you are, boy, but this genocide doesn't concern you," Lord Neff said, laying his gaze upon Kip. It had felt like darkness was surrounding him—making Kip feel alone and cold.

The lord looked straight at Lancer, with those devilish eyes. "You youngsters think you know everything. Coming into my home and barking demands. Why are you so quiet all of a sudden?" The Lord asked her with a twinkle in his hollow eye.

Their eyes met, the Lord wearing the half-mask to hide his rotting face.

"Neff?" Lancer said softly.

A sinister smile exposed the lord's rotten teeth in his festering mouth.

Without hesitation, the blade was back in the Lord's hands.

Luckily Lancer was fast in her own right and punched him in the throat with her stump hand.

That was what was different about her—she was missing both of her hands, Kip now remembers.

As the Lord gasped for air, she didn't stop there. One after another, she tenderized his frail body, pushing him back with blow after blow after blow.

"Go get the pits and get as far away as you can. I will destroy him," Lancer yelled between each strike.

Kip scrambled behind his half-breed friend, Barne, who had already gotten started on loading the pits of his people into a half-decent cart.

"Hurry, we don't have much time, and there are a ton of these," Barne said.

Kip stopped mid-stride as something else caught his eye. His face twitched nervously.

"Hello? K?"

Ignoring the mission and everything else around, Kip walked over to the object of his desire. Something he hadn't had for four days now. The addiction runs deep inside his subconscious, only he doesn't know it.

It was a crate filled to the brim with salm root. Before anymore words could be said, the sweet, sweet milky oil numbed his pain, and everything else was lost.

The answers are right before his eyes except he is too blind to see them. Images flash inside his mind of the root always being around, and he recalls constantly purchasing it, yet he never remembers taking it.

Somehow, he is undoubtably using the stuff, and unfortunately...there might not be a time when he wasn't.

Putting an End to the End

"Like your dreams, life cares nothing about how good or bad you've lived, nor does it care about wealth or poverty. In the end, it is about survival of your individuality. In death, you cannot pack your belongings with you, nor your experiences. It's how you're remembered once you're gone that makes you immortal.

"No one remembers me. Instead they see the veneer I present before them, the persona of who I wish I really was. I've been playing pretend for so long that sometimes I, too, forget who I really am. The snake oil of a salesman is sold through lies, but in my case, this salesman has sampled enough of his own product that he started to pull the wool over his own eyes.

"People share news of the highest highs and the lowest lows. The storybooks are equally full of great heroes as much as they are infamous villains. Never a care is had for the mundane, nor the boring.

"Stable happiness is by far the greatest feeling around, yet it is often forgotten—replaced by the extreme counterparts. Some would rather be forgotten than live on through the memories of a tragic demise...because that would mean that they found the peace that they thought they'd lost.

I spent my life selling grand ideas that I had attached to mediocre objects. What I was really selling was always hope. I never thought that perhaps my memory would become overshadowed by my own act." *-Keve, Owner of The Sea Witch's Apothecary, age 55.*

Day Three, 1:30 am: The King of the Castle

The war party's perimeter created a great opportunity for Kip to rush up the great stone steps towards the throne room.

This whole wing of the castle is newly constructed, since it changed ownership. The current king of these lands is notorious for his sense of humor and lucky business transactions, thus he uses the donkey as his family crest.

First of his name, the king is a businessman above all else and not a war king like other rulers. This is why such an attack surprises Kip, along with everyone else. Battles are fought where power is held, and greed is always to blame. Death and mayhem are merely distractions. Normally, when a business king is concerned, enemies will take their grievances to parliament, not literally grind the axe. No profits are being made tonight. This whole thing reeks of revenge.

Inside the cold, dark walls of the inner sanctum of the castle, torch lights flicker—casting shadows against Kip's back. The farther he goes in, the less destruction he hears from the outside battle.

The walls are decorated with fine treasures from distant lands. Ornate suits of armor, porcelain statues, and vivid oil paintings adorn the halls like an art exhibition. This area is normally guarded and completely closed off to the public. Nothing on these walls is normally open for display. These things belong to the king's personal collection.

Kip breaks his stride to take a closer look at a tan suit of armor. It's finely crafted specifically for war in a sandy terrain. The crafter even went as far as to make discharge holes for unwanted sand and dirt to escape out of.

"You can look, but don't stop," Kip reminds himself.

Not knowing what to expect, nor wanting to surprise a man inside his own house, Kip walks slow and steady while holding his hands up in a non-threatening way.

There is a dripping sound echoing from the end of the hall.

"Hello?" His voice bounces back to him with no reply. "I am unarmed." Still there seems to be no one about, just his haunting echo.

Drip.

Squinting and straining his eyes, Kip spies a set of royal guard's armor lying at the entrance to the next room at the end of the hall. These are similar to the normal house guards' except that every chainmail piece is replaced by steel plates, leaving no flesh exposed to stab.

Kip rushes to inspect it further. His fingers

slowly trace the outline of the donkey crest on the steel chest piece. The armor shifts unnaturally.

Drip.

"It's empty," Kip says, looking inside the suit. It clearly wasn't part of some decoration, based on how it is lying there mimicking a human-like pose exactly. *What happened to the person inside?*

"I mean no harm," Kip says, launching to his feet, suddenly on edge. *What if one of those bad guys is here...*

Constantly looking over his shoulder, Kip continues through the entryway and onward to a hall that curves around and spills into the enormous throne room where the water noise seems to be originating.

Drip.

It's getting louder now.

Extravagant donkey statues, paintings, and wood carvings are displayed proudly all over the room. This must be all his custom commissioned pieces. Each one has a unique beauty that is well worth whatever price the king must have paid for such exquisite works of art.

This part of the castle must have the finest collection of master artistry known to exist. He cannot help but ogle the wonderful treasures for what they are—priceless artifacts.

Each corner of the room has a large vase heaped with gold coins. The one in the right corner has been toppled over, spilling its contents all around the entryway.

Kip bends down and picks up a single coin. "This wasn't a robbery."

He looks toward the center of the room. Spears, swords, and halberds lie next to royal guard suits of armor. Like the one in the hall, they too appear to have been hollowed out. Light shimmers off of the wide perimeter of armor that circles the most masterful piece of art of them all—the throne. It is cut out from a single slab of shimmering pink gemstone, with perfect edges and wonderful carvings of hundreds of animal claws, talons, and webbed feet, all dotted and decorated with various gemstones, framing the grand seat.

Sitting on the feathered cushion of the throne is a prune of a man, dried and wrinkled, like dehydrated meat clinging tightly to his bones. On the top of his head lies a modest looking crown resting in a slumped position down his wizened head, covering his eyes.

Drip.

This is the first time Kip has been in the presence of royalty, even if it is more like the inside of a tomb, and not a formal event like a ball or knighting.

"What happened to you?" Kip asks, cringing at the king's visage on the face of the gold coin he picked up. Either the king is much more ancient than depicted on the coins, or all of the moisture has been removed from his body. The one truth that remains is that he is very much dead.

"I guess your luck has finally run out," Kip says softly, feeling strange speaking to a corpse. He bows his head slightly, finally remembering to show his respect.

Stepping over a couple suits of armor, Kip makes his way to the throne.

Drip.

It is hard to tell in his resting state, but it is entirely possible that the king was smiling in his final moments. "It looks like you got the last laugh, didn't you?" Kip says securing the coin in the dead king's coat pocket with a pat.

Instantly, the room fills with a mysterious shrill sound.

Covering his ears, Kip drops to his knees, trying to scan the area for the source of the harshness.

What if it's coming from the undead king? That thought is horrifying to him. He studies the corpse king for any movements, which there are none. Kip never believed in the tales of reborners—or the undead, as some refer to them. They're all just impostures or pranksters trying to get a rise out of the gullible. No, it has to be coming from some place else—some place close.

Turning his eyes to the ceiling, Kip locks eyes with a woman pinned to a mosaic of a donkey up there. Her blood slowly drips to the ground behind the throne.

When his eyes look into her golden orbs, her mouth clamps shut instantly, and the sound abruptly stops.

"Oh, my! Are you okay? Of course you're not...I...don't know what to say."

Her neck twists and turns in an unnatural way, clicking and snapping.

Caught off guard, Kip can't hide his own nervous tic, almost as if her movement is contagious. This woman looks evil, with wispy hair and pale features, but he doesn't want to come off as threatening.

"I...am going to get you down from there,

miss." Kip picks up a halberd from an empty guard and tries to reach the ceiling, but it is no use. She is much too high up.

How did she even get up there?

"The tenth transfusion is complete, and the end is upon us now," the ceiling woman says through unvoiced echoes.

"Uh...I don't know what that means, but know that I *am* trying to save you."

"You're already dead. As am I."

"So...do you want to stay up there?"

The woman's eyes roll into the back of her head, exposing her glowing whites. Her mouth opens wide, exposing sharp teeth, and now there is the return of the wretched sound.

"I am sorry to upset you." No matter how much he presses his hands over his ears, the sound seems to penetrate straight into his brain as it gets louder and louder still.

The remaining vases shatter, spilling coins everywhere.

He has no choice but to flee down the corridor. The sound is following him like a shadow just behind his steps.

Just about the time Kip feels as though he cannot escape the anguish, it abruptly stops, following a loud slashing sound. She must have yelled so loud that her body broke apart.

"The fool king is gone. There are no more royal guards. We are truly on our own. This means only one thing...she was right—we're all dead."

Day Four, 5:00, pm: Silence is Golden

As fast as the inexplicable murdering spree came, it suddenly falls silent. Kip's ears pulsate from missing the loud noises that have been going on for days. It is as if he is no longer used to the quiet of a normal day.

Darkness evaporates off of everything and into the sky above—bringing bright colors back to the dank castle as if breathing life back into it. Before right now, Kip didn't even notice the spell that engulfed the castle and surrounding area. But now that it is gone, it is clear as day-light.

Kip rises to his feet and dusts himself off as if all the dried blood, sweat, dirt, and every-thing else coating his body don't exist. Looking over both of his shoulders, he notices that no one is following his lead—not the elderly woman, or the thief or anyone else that is hid-ing or pretending to be dead.

Is it over? Truly and completely? Kip has to investigate the sudden change. One minute he thought the thing was coming back for him, the next it is almost as if this whole thing never really happened.

Kip doesn't know about the rest of the survivors, but he has gone through way too much to not see how it all unfolds.

The stillness all around emphasizes every piece of broken glass underfoot as he steps out through the hole where the wizard had mysteriously been pulled through.

Outside it's bright, in an eerie sort of way, and quite surreal. There is no howling of pain, no soft sobbing, but also no cheers of victory.

This has gone on far too long. The casualties are much higher than anything he has ever heard of. Even with that notion on the tip of his mind, Kip has to move forward to find an ending for either himself or this day. Someone will tell the tale of the events that have transpired, and that someone is going to be him. Kip will have to remember everything to give their lives meaning, or maybe his own. But one thing is for certain—he won't be taking any salm medicine ever again.

Here in the courtyard, the lightness of day

paints a gruesome picture of the full extent of the horror that the darkness had masked. His eyes are far too dry to shed any more sadness for those whose lives ended much too soon. This is a blood bath, not a victory...even if it is truly over.

Kip keeps repeating the same words over and over again, trying to make some kind of sense of this situation as he passes through the carnage. "Why?"

No one person can possess such a power, not unless they are a god. Yet, he saw it with his own eyes—unless they were deceiving him and this whole thing was an illusion. Unfortunately, he knows that is not the case.

How can he be expected to remember all of this? He needs answers, and hesitantly moves onward, up the great stone stairs. Something horrendous is in store for him, he feels. As he tentatively climbs up the stairs, he spies a thin red line of liquid is dripping down the cracks of each step like a tiny river seen from a bird's-eye view.

A tightness clenches his chest as he approaches the landing. A dangling hand is limply hanging off the top step.

There it is.

Kip pauses to really take in the scene, two steps away from the top.

Defeated and still, mimicking the calmness in the air, is the gold-robed wizard's body.

"He fell... But...how?" Kip approaches the unmistakable robes, making sure he keeps as far away from them as possible—hugging the far wall just to be safe.

When he had approached the wizard in the temple, Kip had no plan or course of action. Maybe he was going to talk things out, but the truth is more likely that it would have just been assisted suicide. At any rate, anything is better than doing nothing.

Unfortunately, that is exactly what he ended up doing. If it wasn't for the mysterious hook weapon that dragged the wizard out of the window, Kip's life would have surely gone out as fast as the flash from the wizard's hands.

It was in that moment that Kip wanted to live again. He knew he was way over his head. So, he just stood there as the battle carried on outside, across the castle's garden, and continued up the grand stairwell at the foot of the throne room.

The wizard used all the powers he had in his arsenal. Kip remembers hearing them well. It was a one-on-one battle, and he did nothing to help. In what world would that be a fair fight for anyone? One against a god? But that is what it sounded like from inside of the temple's thin walls.

He just played dead and thought of her, the one he abandoned. How could he face her, or withstand the guilt of maybe finding her body? Humiliated and ashamed, he had felt worse than a corpse, worse than a coward. In that moment, he was an insignificant object, not even worth killing.

How did something unkillable, unstoppable, and with unimaginable power get defeated? *Could the wizard have used up all his power and over exhausted himself somehow?*

Making his way up the last two steps, the clues start to fall into place.

The wizard is not in one piece. Something or someone has cut off his head—from the base at the back of his neck to the opposing collar bone. This is not a wound that he could have done to himself. It is jagged and crude, not clean and swift like a normal decapitation. Whatever did this had to have had a strange weapon in order to cut the wizard in such a barbaric way, like the teeth of a huge beast gnashing through his skin and bones.

Something else about this corpse seems familiar to him, but he cannot place it. Kip spins around looking for the victor in the fight, any sign to indicate who or what could have possessed enough power to inflict a blow against such an immeasurable force. All around he looks, but there is nothing there and no indication that anything was ever there.

That would mean that something this powerful still exists out in the world... Then a fearful thought comes to him, *What if I'm next?*

"Hello? Is anyone out there?" His voice echoes through the open area, with no response.

This death isn't at all what the evil wizard deserved. It deserved much, much worse. But it is a victory all the same. The wizard caused so much suffering to so many people, and somehow it seems unfair for him to die from a single wound, no matter how devastating it looks. Even a lifetime of torture wouldn't begin to make up for everything from the past couple of days.

Kip wants to hurt it, to take out all his frustration. He doesn't care if it's dead; he will take what he can get. One strike after another, Kip kicks the corpse, letting it all out. Through gritted teeth, obscenities spill out of his mouth.

Then something stops him dead in his tracks. It's the wizard's head. It's laying on its side...and it is looking at him. The corpse's face shows an expression of sadness that he didn't expect to see. It is deep and everlasting. The stare captures Kip completely.

The truth starts to set in. The wizard pre-paid for his crimes long before this fight. Something awful and chilling must have happened to bring him to such a wicked place. His pain is all in his expression.

What could have pushed the wizard to such a drastic act? Was it a way for him to deal with his misery, or something completely different? Kip starts to feel a pang of sympathy for the man.

"No! You don't get my sympathy. It's not fair!" Kip hates seeing him lying there like a person. He was much better off thinking of him as a supernatural being or a monster, but the truth is far worse—he is only a man, one capable of doing horrible things.

Wait. He looks a little bit familiar.

Kip racks his brain trying to place the mutilated body. *A friend of mine? No, nobody that close.* He tries to recall the voice that matches the corpse, but he can't. He never spoke to him. He would have remembered that.

It's on the fringe of his mind. *Where? Where did I see him?* A distant relative? *Why can't I remember?*

Kip tightens his fists in frustration, straining his mind to focus. Then he remembers the very moment he is looking for. It comes to him not by the wizard's face, but by the sadness exuding from his face.

It is the kind of look that sits with you for a thousand years, far past your own demise and on to the next life to follow. It is through his eye that pounds with emotion where he knew it was him.

He saw this person on the first day of the festival—a small, awkward man, one who was too scared to cross a crowd of people for fear of touching them. Kip wanted to help him or, at the very least, try to. But he was distracted and did nothing. What might have changed if Kip had done something, anything? Could this whole outcome have been avoided? Or would Kip have just been the first victim? Regret is like a sword that shows no mercy.

What pain could have caused him to engage in such acts of brutality? Would I have been capable of such acts if I were in the same situation? Kip fears nothing more than losing control over as himself, among the long list of phobias he has.

He gingerly places his hand on the decapitated head to get a better look upon the face of a slain god.

Kip jumps three feet in the air upon seeing the other side of his face that was against the floor. It is covered in blood and gore. The left eye has been removed right out of its socket.

Something else is not right about this wizard. Dropping the head back where it was, Kip walks over and picks up the wizard's arms, revealing that both of his hands have also been severed off. This also seemed familiar to him somehow.

"What a peculiar wound," a voice observes from behind him.

Both arms flop on the ground, lifeless, as Kip drops them from getting startled.

"Did you do this?" Kip asks the dirt-covered man whose beard is half burnt off.

"No, I thought you did."

"Not I..."

On the ground, there is a grappling hook and rope, the very same one Kip had thrown across the mote.

"It couldn't be," Kip shakes his head in amazement. Without a doubt, he recognizes his janky knot. Except it had been modified somehow with springs and levers in order to turn it into a weapon. Help came, and it was all because of him...

But where are they now? Didn't they want glory and praise? There has to be some reward for stopping a power such as this. Whoever did this is a true hero. They bested the best, stopped the end of the world and just walked away. But like the wind, whatever or whoever did this is gone, already off on another adventure.

Most of all, Kip wishes it could have been him who had done it, but he didn't even think that killing the wizard could be possible. Such a feat of greatness—one used for good, not for glory.

I only saved a goat. What a pitiful hero I am in comparison.

Out of the ash and blood, one by one, those that were hidden come out of their shelter to form a crowd around Kip, who is kneeling over the end of the world's ender.

He wants answers, though they are not

coming easily to him. Some mysteries are never solved, no matter how much you demand the universe to give you the insight you crave.

After truly thinking he was one of the few ones left alive, his heart soars at the thought of all these people surviving such a heinous act. He doesn't have to mourn alone.

The wounded, the half dead, the unscathed, men, women, children, the elderly, all different bloodlines stand together to witness the resolution. Among the masses are a couple of faces he recognizes, though he doesn't know their names—the elderly woman who nearly got trampled, the limping youth who wouldn't let Kip save him, the parchment vendor who was stationed next to Kip, the bone-armored warrior, and the woman with the flower in her hair who is holding on to her no longer lost husband tightly, as if she will never let him go again, not even for a second.

One by one, he recognizes the hopeful faces that start to come out of the woodwork and surround the wicked corpse. Only then does Kip realize that he did have a hand in saving people. Maybe he wasn't the strongest, fastest, or most cunning fighter, but his hope alone gave people the power to survive, the power to rise up and face their tormentor or gather each other to safety. And the evidence is standing and breathing before him.

If the savior of the castle didn't need praise for their efforts, neither does he. Kip spits at the corpse and, one by one, everyone else follows suit.

Kip wasn't the last to survive these most tragic of days, not by far. He may be a coward, but in this moment, he is brave enough to give everyone the courage to stand again, by his side, and quite literally spit on the face of evil.

Day Three Hundred and Sixty-Five: Reunion

No matter who or what they were before the catastrophic event, through togetherness and tragedy, they are family, from now until always. It is a bond thicker than skin, stronger than blood.

In the bosom of a pack, humankind is more resilient than they ever knew, giving more time, money, and love than any bloodline. With perspective comes compassion, and with time comes knowledge.

Today is the anniversary of the event that

almost ended the world. Painters, sculptors, poets, and many other artists have come from across the lands to decorate the gravesites—depicting each victim in their final resting place. The detail that they put in their works makes the King's art hoard look like finger paintings in comparison.

Not one victim is overlooked in the artistry. Even those cowering inside their hiding places are represented as heroes, for every life is given the time and attention it deserves.

This is the start of what will become a long-lived tradition from a place of beauty and deep meaning. The art brings people from near and far to pay their respects to those that gave their lives so that others may live. The once great castle is now a living graveyard, educating through compassionate hearts. This is now a place of healing, respect and endless beauty. Every single day, tears drizzle on the cobblestone grounds where 873 people lost their lives in just 36 hours. The tears are both of joy and sadness. For this is a place of art and play, where all are welcome to express themselves freely without limitation, as well as to remember those who made the ultimate sacrifice.

As for Kip, this is the first year that he's been

clean from the salm root narcotic. He had been addicted to it for nearly his whole life and didn't even know it. The purpose had always been forgetting pain, but the side effect was forgetting everything else, even taking the substance itself. Being rid of the stuff has helped him see the world in perfect clarity for the first time in his life. No longer are his memories and timelines all mixed up; he is free.

His whole family came far and wide to be a part of this emotional event. They even forgave him for stealing jewels and fleeing their homeland to buy more salm when they tried to make him quit.

Kip's new motto is that one should always share upward progress, for it will raise your spirit and others' along with it. So, he acts as a success story for substance abuse, going to great lengths to help ban the drug in many major developing territories. Kip is at the heart of everyone's healing, acting as the glue that repairs all the pain that has transpired inside their broken hearts.

Every man, woman, elder, or child who was slain that day will be remembered on the wall of heroes. Pride and respect will be forever intertwined with their surnames, and praises and love are whispered to the guardian angels within earshot.

All but one name is accounted for to be remembered. His identity and title are stripped away—erased from history so that he cannot live on in infamy. Not even spit is allowed to be spent for his misdeed.

This person deserves no fear and no praise, only nothingness. He is the one who caused all the destruction, all the sorrow. He is the one who came without explanation or reason, only to hurt and harm. The very one that made the largest gravesite in all of the tarnished lands. He will now and forever be simply known as "The One." The one without a legacy. The one without soul. The one to be forgotten so that no one will follow in his stead.

Still, to this very day, on the anniversary of the horrible event, most do not even know why it started or how it ended. All they know is that the world almost lost itself forever.

But buried deep within those tragic days, Kip found himself and who he is, not who he wanted to be. In turn, he also found a loving wife. The very woman he rescued and kept safe in the sewers. Every now and again, he catches himself still lost in her wonderous gaze. On their wedding day, he not only vowed to love her completely for himself, but for everyone else that lost a loved one, and to continue until forever. That is one promise he never broke.

The End

ABOUT THE AUTHOR

After surviving an almost fatal car accident directly in front of a bookstore, P.A. Wikoff decided not to ignore the sign and proceeded to self-publish his work. Mr. Wikoff kick-started his writing career by releasing the epic fantasy novel "Feylin Lore: Reflections." When P.A. is not writing, he spends all of his free time with his beautiful wife and two fabulous kids who inspire him every single day.

A Fantasy/Romance Novel

"Complex Fantasy Romance"
"The story is very well written. From the beginning, I was sucked in and it was hard to
put it down. The story is interesting and
quite complex. There is adventure, danger,
suspense, humor, and romance. Narration
was well done and brought the story to life.
There is a lot of detail and unique character
development. There are also quite a few
twists and turns to throw us off. I had to listen to most of it with little distraction
because there is so much going on that you
need to focus or you will miss something important. Everything happens at a good pace
though, not too fast or too slow. I was given
this free review copy audiobook at my request and have voluntarily left this review."
- Adriana B

A Single-Author Collection

ANTHOLOGY
OF SCROLLS
P.A. WIKOFF

Review for Anthology of Scrolls.
"Splashes of engaging poetry are sprinkled
in between some of the most extraordinary,
thought-provoking, short-stories.
Each story immediately draws me in, pulling me deep into a relatable, yet mind-
bending plot-line. As I crawl into each character's mind, I'm taken on a new, sometimes
mysterious adventure. Then, it's wrapped
up to its end. Leaving me desiring more in
only the best of ways. So many questions
and creative energy spring forth in my
mind. These stories make you consider
things, you may have never given a second
thought too. If you enjoy Black Mirror or
The Twilight Zone, then you will definitely
love this book. I know that I will be thinking
on many of these stories and tales for a long,
long time! I really recommend that you
check out this book. It is so unique and different from the majority of the books out
there. The author has a way of making
mundane sentences hilarious or making or-
dinary conversation suspicious.
I will be looking forward to see what else
will come from this author in the future." -
D.G. Alan

As a new author, it's extremely difficult to get started without the support of a marketing team and publisher. The make/break point for self-published authors is honest reviews.

If you could take a couple of minutes to leave a review on Amazon and/or Goodreads, (even a line or two), it would be greatly appreciated.

Thank you so much!
-PA

www.ingramcontent.com/pod-product-compliance
Lightning Source LLC
Chambersburg PA
CBHW072011110726
47910CB00005B/1718